SWINDLED

A CHANCY ROSMAN WESTERN ADVENTURE
BOOK 2

Russell J. Atwater

Contents

Chapter 1
Firefight

Frank McFarland was tired. But not simply fatigued. Not worn out. He was irritated, angry. He was ready to tear Elkhorn apart with his own two hands. Provided, of course, he could get his hands on the keys to the cell door.

It had been thirteen days since he'd been tossed in the cramped, hot, filthy cell. The room wasn't even half the size of his office. The wooden cot and thin blanket made sleep almost impossible, and the food... he wouldn't even subject the dogs on the ranch to such trash. They even called it chow.

"You don't even attempt civility here, do you? Perhaps you can't?" Frank had asked after his first few meals.

"Being civil ain't what got you in here," the deputy responded.

"It's not what made me rich, either." Frank grinned. He'd been certain he could turn one of the green deputies. A man's integrity was never as strong as he thought.

But the guard merely stood there, holding out the tin dish. "I ain't gotta make ya eat it. I just gotta give ya the option."

Frank looked at the man, realizing the slight protest of a skipped meal would mean nothing at all. "I could put a steak on your plate every night, you know," he said, taking the dish.

"I'm sure you could," the man said, walking off. "But I don't know who'd end up paying for it."

Frank scoffed, tearing at the hard bread, attempting to sop it in the beans. And so, it had gone for nearly every meal since.

But what put acid in his heart, what made him toss and turn and pace the tiny cell at all hours of the night and day, was that he was still there. Thirteen days and he'd had one visitor—a rangy young man McFarland had brought on as only a glorified butler at his home.

If it hadn't been for regularly seeing the youth slink around the stables and bunkhouse, Frank would've likely forgotten who the young man even was. McFarland ran his life efficiently and couldn't be expected to keep track of every shiftless face that passed through.

With Thomas, though, Frank had been forced to sit up and pay attention. Though in all actuality, whether Thomas was the man's first or last name, McFarland did not know. The point was, out of all the people he'd made rich in his long life, Thomas was the only one proving to be more than a fair-weather friend. Which was miles beyond what Frank could say about that useless woman, Anne-Marie.

Surely, she'd made plans, and probably tracks, before Frank had been brought in. He certainly didn't recall seeing her the day of his arrest. She had just better pray her path took her to some dark hole Frank couldn't find because he had a short list of things on his mind.

The first was to get out of this forsaken hole. The second was to burn Elkhorn to the ground. And somewhere in there, Anne-Marie was owed a long, painful visit.

As Frank stared out the barred window at the barren nothingness behind the jail, one of the new deputies came up and banged on the cell door behind him. That Rosman fellow had been by a time or two, though not nearly as much as Frank had expected.

There had been no gloating, practically no interaction at all between the two. Rosman had answered questions and provided information, and as far as anything else was concerned, the sheriff had left it to the deputies.

Ironic, Frank thought. Now that they locked him up, now that the major threat to the town had been neutralized, now was the time Travis bulked up the number of lawmen. Perhaps it was flattering, in a way.

Frank had shown the town how weak it was, how vulnerable. Unfortunately, it had made any attempt at getting out of the jail nearly impossible. His attempts to manipulate the law had fallen flat, and the deputies were as straight as Rosman himself.

Where Travis had found the men, Frank couldn't imagine. Two weeks ago, the town had been in his pocket. Now, suddenly, McFarland couldn't buy a friend.

"Visitor," the deputy said, unlocking the steel door and letting Thomas in.

Well, Frank thought, any port in a storm.

"Ten minutes," the deputy said, wandering back off toward the front of the station.

Thomas stood by the door, still showing signs of intimidation. That was good. Perhaps Thomas wasn't a friend, but he continued to show signs of, if not loyalty, at least an obligation to the businessman. "I tried to bring ya some grub," Thomas said, "but they ain't havin' it. Probably up there eatin' it they own selves right now."

Frank smiled. Perhaps the scales did indeed tilt more toward dedication in the man. "Undoubtedly," Frank said, sitting down on the cot. "It's reprehensible the way they treat a man in this town. And for what? Attempting to breathe some life into a struggling economy? For reaching out a helping hand to those in need?"

"Shameful," Thomas said.

"You see," Frank replied. "You understand what I was trying to accomplish."

The look on Thomas's face made his comprehension questionable, but there the man stood, and it was more than Frank could say about anyone else he'd invested in. Perhaps Thomas deserved a little more responsibility.

"Thomas," Frank began, then paused. Perhaps overdramatically, Frank moved to the cell door.

Thomas hunkered back, as if from a strange dog.

Funny, Frank thought. He'd never struck the man, at least not that he could recall. Violence by his own hand had always been off-putting. Then again, his hired men often interpreted orders in their own, more base ways, so a word from Frank could very well have been what made the man so skittish.

After theatrically checking the hall in both directions, Frank gestured to the man to come sit next to him on the cot. Thomas, with some reluctance, took a seat at the edge of the bed.

"Thomas," Frank began again. "You've proven yourself to be an exceptional man in the last few weeks. I want you to know that I've noticed that, and that loyalty to me does not go unrewarded."

The man looked down, still appearing unsure, but the hint of a smile played at the corners of his mouth.

"The situation we find ourselves in now is more than unpleasant," Frank continued, "but I have good reason to believe it's also a temporary one. Of course, if I can rely on you?"

"Oh, 'course, sir," Thomas said. "Far as I know, I'm still employed by you, no matter where you're sleepin' at."

"Good man," Frank said. "I knew I could count on you. Now I need you to listen closely because I'm going to need you to do a special job for me. At the moment, our team is sparse, and we need to recruit some more hands. When you leave here today, this is what I need you to do."

Thomas listened, repeated the information to McFarland, and in nine minutes, left.

***

Two days later, Chancy sat heavily in the chair across from his desk, a deputy occupying Rosman's regular seat. The man, Jack Wallace, stood, but Chancy waved him off.

"Just catching my breath," Chancy said. "I swear, I thought things'd settle down once we got Frank in here. Seems like they're getting worse every day."

Wallace, a taciturn man who'd taken part in the rescue of Teresa and simply begun showing up at the sheriff's office afterward, shrugged. "No one's leading the gang anymore. Every man for himself."

"Maybe," Chancy said. "But this isn't like what it was before. You remember. Last time it was random. Gun fights, brawls. McFarland was trying to wear us out by spreading us thin."

"You mean you."

Chancy sighed. "Sure. But the point is, this isn't like that. I don't mean to sound nervous, but this seems a little more targeted. We ain't going out to haul in drunks. The drunks are coming after us."

Wallace nodded. "Reckon there's a reason for that."

Chancy looked up at the man. "What've you heard?"

"Rumors so far," Wallace said. "Was waiting for you to come back in."

"Rumors tend to have some truth," the sheriff said.

"What I figured, too. Word I been hearing is our boy," Wallace gestured with his head back toward the cells, "is fixing to get on outta here."

"How?" Chancy asked. "His crew, what was left of it anyway, scattered when we brought him in."

Wallace shrugged. "Always folks lookin' to pick up extra work, assuming the pay's good. And if it ain't all hogwash, it sounds like the pay's pretty good."

"How much?"

"Twenty grand."

Chancy took off his hat and ran a hand through his hair. He let out a low whistle and looked at the deputy. "If it was anybody else, I'd say it was malarkey. Ain't nobody got twenty grand lying around to just toss out like that."

"Nobody but Frank McFarland," Wallace said.

"Or at least," Chancy mused, "I wouldn't believe it if it was anybody but Frank McFarland. I'm sure the man's got more hidey-holes than a squirrel, but twenty thousand is a lot to hide. Any idea if it's true?"

Wallace leaned forward, folding his hands on the desk. "Way I see it, Chance, it don't matter if it's true or not. What matters is if folks'll believe it. And from what you and me been seein', they believe it. You say you think they're making it personal, and I think you're hittin' the nail on the head. Right now they're feelin' us out. Splittin' us up, seein' what we'll do. But that ain't gonna last. You and me both know McFarland ain't gonna sit in here much longer before somebody makes a move like they done before."

Chancy thought back to the man who'd sat in that very seat not three weeks ago, a man who'd lost his life at the whim of one of McFarland's gang. If those men had been willing to kill to send a message, there was no telling what they'd do for twenty thousand dollars. The sheriff looked over at the man. "We've only got one move then."

"Get him out of here?"

"Exactly." Chancy leaned forward to the desk and spun a sheet of paper around to face himself, writing out a brief message. "McFarland's supposed to stay with us till we send him off to trial, but I think we got what ya might call extenuating circumstances. Run down to the telegraph office and send this to the marshals. It's a request for transfer as soon as possible."

"On it, boss." Wallace took the paper and headed toward the door.

"And be careful," Chancy said. "These stars are lookin' a lot more like targets lately."

Jack Wallace nodded and headed outside.

Chancy sat for a moment in the chair, considering his options. Of course, pondering would only get one so far. And why think about things when one could just go to the source? He stood up, his knees cracking from fatigue, and sauntered down the hall toward the cells.

"Well, well," McFarland said, approaching the bars of the cell door. "We have spent little time reacquainting ourselves, Sheriff. I was so hoping to spend more time together."

Chancy leaned against the wall across from the man, a boot up behind him, his arms crossed. "You haven't been leaving me much time for pleasantries," the sheriff said.

McFarland attempted an innocent expression. Perhaps true to his character, the one thing the slippery businessman couldn't approximate was a purely honest face. "I can't imagine what you mean," he said. "I've been here for over two weeks now. Surely you aren't implying I'm running some kind of criminal enterprise while you house me. You barely allow me visitors, not that the list is long these days, anyway."

"You trying to make me feel bad for you?" Chancy laughed. "You oughtta be happy we haven't been allowing you too many visitors. Most folks who come by to see Frank McFarland ain't wantin' to shake your hand."

"You make my point," McFarland said. "So, unless you think I'm sending smoke signals out this pathetic window you've allotted me, I'm afraid your suspicions must be ungrounded."

Chancy sighed, smiling. "Frank, Frank, Frank. Someday you gotta learn you can't con everybody. And it's doubly hard to do when it's the sheriff in charge of the cell you're standing in. I don't know how most folks react to you, but I don't forget those who tried to have me shot."

"Oh, if you're referring to that unfortunate incident with Mrs. Slayton, I stand by my previous statements. Bring me the man you claimed I hired, and we can all discuss whatever misunderstanding has occurred. Oh…" Frank smiled. "I'm sorry. You shot that man in the throat, didn't you? Shame. He could've been extremely helpful in your case."

Chancy knew Frank was baiting him. He'd grown used to it, though it was also part of the reason he avoided talking to the prisoner. Every minute he spent with the man made the idea of stepping into the cell and having it out more and more appealing.

"I suppose that's a risk you take when you draw down on a fella," Chancy said. "Course, you stay far away from that side of things."

Frank smiled. "If you're trying to insult me by pointing out that I find more mature and adult ways to handle my problems, I'm afraid you'll be disappointed."

"Mature and adult, huh? That's the way you see it?" Chancy said. "Because sounds to me like all you do—all you've ever done—is pay somebody to take care of your problems for you."

"Well, that's an interesting way to put it, coming from a man paid to take care of problems."

Chancy smiled. "Let's just cut to the chase, Frank. I know about the twenty grand. What I wanna know is, are you bluffing? Seems to me you don't have a whole lot waiting on you outside this cell, besides an angry town and some US Marshals. So even if somebody took you up on the offer, you're going to have to do some fancy dancing to keep yourself from catching a bullet when you can't pay up."

Frank walked over and sat on the cot, leaning back against the wall with his hands behind his head. "I assure you I don't have the slightest idea what you are discussing here," he said. "I can only say that, purely from a business perspective, from an *imagined* business perspective, one will never get far on bluffs. I don't know what you've been hearing from the little hooligans and rabble-rousers out there, but I know I never make an offer I can't back up."

Chancy thought for a moment, looking down the hall. "Well, Frank, I don't reckon we're gonna find. I just came down to let you know that, because of unrest in the town, we're keeping an extra special eye on making sure you stay safe, so there ain't gonna be no more visits for the time being."

"How noble." Frank smiled.

"I know I'm wasting my breath," Chancy said, "but if there's anything you wanna come clean about, now'd be the time."

"I simply sit here and wait, as per your instruction," Frank replied. "I can't imagine what I have to confess to you."

"What I figured," Chancy said. "Have a pleasant night."

Chancy walked back up the hall to his desk, reaching the main office just as Wallace returned from the telegraph office around the corner.

"What's the word?" Chancy asked.

"Well..." Jack held out a slip of paper. "Good and bad, I reckon. Marshals say they'll come get 'im early, but we still got three days afore they can make it."

Chancy took the paper Jack handed him and skimmed the lines. "Well—"

Just then, the thunder of galloping horses tore past the building, whoops and gunfire ringing out in accompaniment. Jack and Chancy exchanged a look.

"Gonna be a long seventy-two hours," Jack said as the pair headed toward the door.

***

Two nights later, Wallace and Rosman found themselves back at the desk again, this time with Chancy in the sheriff's seat. The pair were tired, having done their best to split shifts over the last forty-eight hours. Chancy trusted all three of his new deputies, but there was something about Wallace that set the sheriff a little more at ease than the others. Perhaps it was Wallace's calm, his quietness. The man seemed sure of himself while also very aware of the dangers the job presented. The other two men, Clay Blount and Burl Newcom, Chancy knew were willing to fight for him, knew they were good men. But if his back was against the wall, Jack Wallace was the one he wanted by his side.

"You oughtta get home and get some rest," Chancy said. "You've had a hard couple days."

"Ah…" Jack stretched out his legs in front of him. "Only terrible thing about a problem is when you don't know when it'll end. This problem oughtta wind up in"—he checked his pocket watch—"twelve, fourteen hours. Shoot, by the time I get home, get to bed, and get back, all the excitement could be over."

Chancy smiled and gestured toward his eye, where on Wallace the deep blues and purples of a shiner stood out. "How's that feeling?"

"Oh, this?" Wallace grinned. "Plumb forgot about it."

"Right." Chancy gestured to his own split lip. "Me too."

The last two days had been rough, though in a way, Chancy found them oddly exhilarating. Since McFarland's crew had scattered, the remaining roughnecks in the town were unorganized. And without a leader, they were ill prepared. Attacks were sloppy, not clearly thought out. Truth be told, after what Chancy had experienced in his days as a bounty hunter, the interactions he and his men had been dealing with ranked little higher than skirmishes. Most felt more like misunderstandings.

What concerned him most, however, and what made him doubly appreciative of Jack's resolve to see things through, was the ticking clock. He and his deputies had done their best to keep Frank's early departure within the office walls.

Even the man himself was unaware. Or at least, Chancy thought, he knew neither he nor Jack had spread word. But as the saying goes, the only way for a secret to stay kept is if nobody knows it.

Not that he didn't trust his men, but he knew men talked. To friends. To girlfriends. To wives, or wives-to-be as with at least one of his new deputies, despite the explicit request the men be unattached. He'd known from the get-go word would get out. But as Wallace had said, if they could make it till morning, they should be all right.

As if on cue, one of the front windows of the sheriff's office shattered. A glass bottle burst on the floor, flames immediately blanketing the area in a blue-orange heat.

Without a word, both Chancy and Wallace hit the floor, and before Chancy could make a move, he saw Wallace crawling toward the cells. Despite the immediate need for action, Chancy had time to be thankful for Jack yet again. The deputy was headed for the blankets stored in the back closet.

Chancy moved up toward the front of the building, to the side opposite the pool of flames. Wedging his back into the corner, he could just barely catch a glimpse out through the remaining intact window. The glow of the fire combined with the darkness outside put him at a distinct disadvantage. He could see hardly anything, but whoever had thrown the bottle had a perfect view of what was happening inside.

Just then, Wallace slipped back into the room. He was moving in a low crouch, a bundle of blankets in his arms that he tossed ahead of him, covering the burning liquid and smothering the flames effectively. Within just a few moments, he'd gotten the situation under control and was kneeling in the corner opposite Chancy, gun drawn, the barrel pointing up next to his black eye. "Guess I might stick around," Jack said, grinning over at Chancy.

"Much obliged," Chancy said, almost laughing despite himself. Yes, this reminded him more his bounty hunting days. "Can you see anything out your side? I can't see nothing but myself in this glass."

Before Jack could reply, a voice called out from the darkness. "Y'all know what we're after, so let's not make a big to-do of it. Give us Frank, and we'll let ya live."

Chancy looked over at Jack, eyebrows raised. Jack shook his head.

"We'll give ya two minutes to think it over," the unfamiliar voice called again. "After that, offer's expired, and we'll just come get 'im ourselves."

Chancy watched as Jack slowly shifted toward the broken window, attempting to get a better view through the opening. The deputy held up three fingers, pointed toward Chancy, held up another, then, at the crack of a gunshot, ducked back into the corner.

Three men on my side, Chancy thought, *one in the middle. May as well figure at least another two or three on Jack's side. Six on two at best.* He looked over at Jack, who was calmly crouched in the corner of the walls, awaiting instruction.

Chancy flipped the gun in his hand, holding it by the barrel and using the butt to smash out the glass next to him. He saw Jack grinning and shrugged.

"I'm not sure you fellas thought this one through," Chancy yelled out to the men. "Seems maybe you oughtta be takin' them two minutes to use as a head start before Blount and Newcom show up."

The two lawmen could hear laughter from outside, though the mixing of voices gave them no further clue who their assailants could be. Chancy risked a quick glance out into the darkness. Just as he'd expected. He pointed to Jack and held up three fingers. The man raised his eyebrows and palms as if to say, "fine."

Fine, perhaps, but what Chancy didn't like was the organization. Clearly, one man was spearheading this, and that was precisely what the sheriff had been depending on not happening. Chancy knew he was a fast draw and a deadly shot. Jack had proven nearly his match. But the two of them hunkered down inside the building made easy targets.

"One minute," the voice called again.

"You out there, Randall?" Jack hollered from his spot.

Chancy shot him a glance, and Jack just shrugged.

"Worth a shot," the deputy mumbled.

There was a murmur of voices from outside, making Chancy wonder if Jack's guess had in fact been right on the mark. The sound of hooves concerned him more though. For him and Jack to have any chance, the men needed to stay close together, grouped up where confusion and space would work against the outlaws and in the favor of the lawmen.

If the men spread out around the building, this could turn into a dark night for Jack and Chancy. He looked over at Jack, the man's demeanor as relaxed as if they were shooting the breeze over dinner at the Horseshoe.

"Time's about up," the man outside yelled.

"Yeah, yeah," Chancy hollered back. "I just wanted to make sure you had every chance to change your mind before you caught a bullet. Helps me sleep better."

The voice laughed. "I come through that door; you'll be sleeping for good."

"Aw, you can do better than that," Chancy yelled, hoping to buy some time, even if, and perhaps especially because, it would irritate the man. Cool heads planned; angry ones acted. Seven men rushing the door would be about as foolish a move as one could make, and Chancy hoped, if nothing else, he could taunt them into just such an action.

The silence from outside, however, left him certain the jibes would not work. Chancy looked over at Jack and held up three fingers. "On three," he said to the deputy. "Unless you got a better plan."

Jack grinned. "I was thinkin' about gettin' some grub after this."

Chancy smiled, shaking his head. "One... two..."

A pair of shots broke through the night air. Chancy hunkered back down, looking over at Jack. Outside, the horses whinnied and trampled about. The voices were angry but, more importantly, confused.

Another few shots rang out wildly, the bullets aimed apparently anywhere but at the sheriff's station. Jack was up and through the front door before Chancy had a moment to cover him. *Brave, but maybe a little too brave* Chancy thought, racing out after him.

The scene in the street was remarkable.

The group of men was pushed together, horses jumping unsteadily as their riders tried to regain control. Guns were drawn but pointed haphazardly as the men whipped their heads from side to side, attempting to take in everything except what was happening at their previous target. Jack raced to one end of the wooden porch, taking slim cover behind one beam supporting the roof. Chancy moved to the other end.

Another shot came out of the dark, and one man fell, his cries causing more chaos in the already disorganized group. Chancy was trying to pinpoint where the gunfire had come from when another rang out from what sounded like just above him in the next building over.

Wherever it was, it was enough to break the flimsy control the man held over his posse. Horses broke off in all directions, gunfire now coming steadily from not only the group but the surrounding streets. Chancy whirled around the beam, coming out from cover with his gun drawn, seeing Jack mirror his movement in his peripheral vision. He tried to draw a bead on one of the escaping men, but the darkness and confusion made it impossible to ensure he could bring the man down without killing him outright.

Within seconds, all that was left of the would-be attackers was a cloud of dust and the slowly dying sound of horse hooves. Chancy ran into the middle of the street, heedless of the unseen gunmen. If they'd wanted him dead, they could've just waited and let the gang do their work. "Come out!" Chancy yelled. "Drop your weapons and get out here! Now!"

Before Chancy had time to note the movement, he felt Jack's back press up against his. "You better hope they's on our side," Chancy heard the man mutter.

"Reckon we'd already be dead if they ain't."

He felt the man shrug, the logic apparently good enough for Jack Wallace.

"C'mon now!" Chancy hollered again.

Finally, after a few seconds of silence, they heard the first voice call out from the shadows. "Take it easy, boys. We're with you all."

"Who's we?" Jack said.

Out of the shadows off to Chancy's left, a form appeared, a rifle held high in one hand, the other empty and raised in the moonlight as well. "Just us concerned citizens." The figure approached, slowly letting the gun fall to his side.

Chancy laughed and walked up to meet him, a hand extended. "Working awful late tonight, aren't ya, Mr. Nichols?"

"You know how it is in the mercantile business." The man smiled. "Gotta stay abreast of things."

As Chancy looked around, two more men appeared from the darkness, one from an alley just down from the sheriff's office, another from across the street.

"I gotta say, I'm rather thankful that's the case," Jack said, walking up and clapping the man on the shoulder.

Mr. Nichols shrugged. "You fellas ain't the only ones who prefer town a little calmer."

"How's your boy?" Chancy said, walking with the man as the small group moved back to the light of the sheriff's building.

"Fine, fine," Mr. Nichols said. "Runnin' around like you'd never know anything'd happened. Though I reckon you see him as much as I do."

Chancy grinned. "He seems to be seeing an awful lot of Betsy these days, doesn't he?"

***

The following morning, Frank McFarland sat in the stifling heat, hands and ankles shackled, his last view of the town coming through the small, barred window on the back of the marshal's wagon. One guard stood at the wooden door, gun drawn, eyes scanning the streets, while the businessman whispered to him through the opening. Chancy watched from his desk chair, the wind blowing freely through the broken window.

"Seems like you boys have a friendly town on your hands here then," the marshal across from him said.

"They're trying," Chancy said. "You sure you trust that man out there? I'm telling ya right now, McFarland makes some slick deals."

The marshal smiled. "That man is my brother-in-law," he said. "He already knows he's on thin ice with me."

Chancy laughed. "Poor Frank don't know what he's up against."

The marshal stood. "No, Sheriff, I don't believe he does. With all due respect, however"—he gestured with his hat toward the windows and the pile of blankets still smelling of smoke— "do you?"

Chancy looked up at him. "I reckon one of my major concerns is no longer in my jurisdiction. As for them fellas who come by last night, I'd say they got a simple message that folks here aren't interested in buying what they're selling."

"You're in a delicate spot now, though," the marshal said. "Seems to be an opening here for a new crime boss."

"Fine by me." Jack crossed the room and sat down on the edge of the desk. "They keep showing up, we keep runnin' em out, and sooner or later, they'll get the message."

The marshal looked over at the deputy, the slightest trace of displeasure at Wallace's bravado clear in the man's eyes.

"And we will keep you abreast of things." Jack smiled.

"You do that," the marshal said. "For now, we've got a man to transport. We appreciate your help and wish you the best in apprehending your posse."

"Much obliged," Chancy said, standing to shake the man's hand. "But like I said, you keep an eye on that fella. He's still pretty sure he's gonna find a way outta this one."

"That," the marshal said, looking at Jack, "is something I'd like to see."

Chancy watched as the man walked back out to the wagon, made a few comments to his brother-in-law, and then the pair mounted the seat at the front of the wagon, leaving town in a small plume of dust.

***

Not terribly far from where Chancy and Jack stood in the sheriff's office, a sheet of paper describing the marshal's movements sat on a finely polished oak desk.

"He's theirs until the trial," a man said.

"That's fine. We can let him stew a while longer." Anne-Marie smiled. "Perhaps he'll be a bit more humble this time around."

Chapter 2
Teresa's Predictions

A few nights later, Chancy was reclining in his favorite chair, the one on the porch at Teresa Slayton's boarding house.

The night was dark and quiet. Betsy had gone off to bed, and Chancy and Teresa were enjoying their evening ritual of iced tea as they traded stories from the day. A cool breeze blew in from the flat land, bringing an extra bit of comfort to Chancy's tired body.

"I know it makes me sound like a doomsday preacher," Teresa was saying, "but after what happened with Frank... well, if you hadn't been there to rescue me out at that shack, I don't know what would've happened."

Chancy folded his hands in his lap, thinking, not for the first time, about the close call he and Teresa had experienced that afternoon not so long ago. "That was a pretty tight spot," he said, attempting to ease her mind with a confidence he wasn't sure he'd felt.

Before, when he'd been on his own, he would've laughed the incident off and likely found himself staring down another gun within a day or two. The bounty hunter's life he'd led had been fast-paced, dangerous, and, if he was to be honest, exciting.

Something about following a trail, putting his wits and skill up against those on the run, often those with nothing to lose, had kept his blood pumping fast. It was something he'd liked, perhaps even loved, about the work.

But part of his last move, a big part of moving to the area, had been an attempt to step away from all that. Chancy was no fool. He knew the longer he drew down on a man, the more the odds tilted against him.

Every gunfight could be his last, and with every day he got older, he would get just a little slower, his eyesight just a little less keen. If it hadn't been from Frank, or perhaps more so Travis, Chancy would've been just fine settling in and not firing his gun every day.

Especially after seeing Teresa at the shack. The look in her eyes, the fear, that was nothing new. At least not given the situation. He'd saved people before, just as he'd shot people before. Those often felt like the two biggest parts of being a bounty hunter.

But there was something different about seeing Teresa that day. He'd been nervous in a way he'd not felt in the past. For a moment, he'd been unsure. And it was the uncertainty that gave him pause.

"I wish I could see it as simply as you do," Teresa said, bringing him out of his thoughts. "Maybe if I'd seen more excitement in my life, I could just write it off as another ordinary day. I'm sure you've had a gun pointed at you more times than you can count.

But—and I'm not ashamed to say it—I was scared that day."

Chancy thought for a moment longer. He'd been scared, too. Not for himself, or at least not entirely. He'd always known the risks he took and often welcomed them. But he'd been scared for her. Scared of what could've happened to Teresa if his hand had been too slow and if his aim had been even slightly off.

The truth was, it had scared him that would be the last time he'd see her, not only because she could've been killed but because he could've as well.

Somehow, and perhaps this was the most unsettling aspect of it all, somehow, he'd grown attached to the woman, to Betsy, to the feelings of normalcy in the boarding house. Sure, he was technically just another paying customer, but the longer he stayed, the more times he came back to dinner or sat with Teresa on the porch, the more this felt like his home.

But attachments meant weaknesses and that, more than anything, was something Chancy wasn't comfortable admitting. At least not yet.

"Travis and his boys had everything under control," he finally said, looking over at the woman. "I know it seemed like things were about to get hot, but I knew they were coming. I just didn't tell you." He grinned.

Teresa eyes him suspiciously. "So you say, Chancy Rosman. So you say."

He shrugged. "We're sitting here now. Seems to me like it all worked out."

The woman sighed. "You cowboys. Not a care in the world, is that right?"

"Well, now, I didn't say that."

"No, no," her tone took on a teasing note. "I understand. I wouldn't want anyone to find out their cold-blooded sheriff had a soft spot."

Chancy tried to smile, though he felt his cheeks redden just a bit. She could always read him, and this had been too close to his own thoughts for comfort. "I have an image to keep."

"About that," Teresa said. "As I was saying, I don't want to be all doom and gloom, but have you thought about what's going to happen now that Frank is officially gone? At least for now."

"At least for now?"

The woman laughed softly. "Chancy, I sometimes think you forget I've been here longer than you. You may've seen more of the world, but I've seen more of this town. What happened with Frank was... well, it was certainly on a scale we've not seen before. But that's not to say it was unusual."

Chancy thought for a moment.

Teresa leaned forward and looked over at him. "I wondered..." She smiled, then continued, "When you spend your whole life riding from place to place, I'm sure you see a lot of things. And I suppose that gives you some advantages a person like me wouldn't have. But don't think you aren't sacrificing some things for others. You're never around long enough to see the patterns, Chancy. Sure, you know there are always evil men, and you go bring them in. But if you're here today and gone tomorrow, you never see what happens next. This isn't a bedtime story. There's never a happily ever after."

"There's only what's next, huh?"

"Yes," she said. "Or who. I've been hoping you would stay because... well, for a lot of reasons." Chancy thought he saw just the hint of a blush on her cheek. "But one of them is what happens next. You took Frank McFarland down, and we thank you for that. But by doing that, you also left an opening. I'm not saying being the local outlaw is a profession, but it certainly works that way often."

"So, your guess is it's just a matter of time before someone else steps up."

Teresa leaned back in her rocking chair. "That's the way it's always been. And Frank was a bit more, shall we say, successful than others in the past. But just because one man is with the marshals now doesn't mean another won't step up to take his place. In fact, it almost guarantees it."

Chancy chewed on her words. They made sense. And unfortunately for his pride, at least, she made a strong point. He never had stuck around anywhere too terribly long.

He had a goal, a person to track down, a problem to solve, and he did that. And then he moved on to the next place with some money to offer. Staying in one place hadn't appealed to his wandering sensibilities any more than it had to his pocketbook.

But now, here, it wasn't the money that concerned him. He'd been smarter than most in his youth, and the money would never be an issue. What bothered him now was someone undoing what he'd worked so hard to accomplish. What bothered him more was the idea of someone threatening the people he cared about.

"I hear what you're saying," he finally said, "and I can tell you this: I don't have any plans on going anywhere any time soon. If somebody decides they wanna be the next Frank McFarland, well, I guess they know what they're up against. I will tell you though, Teresa, you didn't see what I seen the other night. Me and Jack weren't in the best of positions when the boys showed up at the office. But it was Mr. Nichols and the rest that really made the move. It ain't just me and you hoping this place will turn out for the better."

"I hope you're right," she said.

Chancy started to say something then caught himself. "We got good folks in this town. The important thing is that they're realizing it as well."

She looked over at him, an eyebrow raised.

"What?"

She smiled. "I don't know if you've ever said we before. You're getting attached to..." She reddened again. "This place."

Chancy swirled the remaining tea in his glass, looking down. "It's a good place," he said.

After a pause, Teresa stood up and moved to the door. "Well, we enjoy having you here, so you keep what I said in mind. I might be completely wrong, and I hope I am, but you don't get too comfortable in that desk chair. Someone will step up to try you eventually, and I've gone and grown accustomed to having you here. So, keep your wits about you."

"Yes, ma'am." He smiled as she walked inside.

***

Over the next few weeks, Teresa's predictions had proven themselves true several times. There had been no new Frank McFarland, to Chancy's relief. He wasn't scared of another big gun coming to town, but the fact was, he simply wasn't in the mood to deal with it.

His peaceful life had been ravaged enough when he first pinned on the sheriff's star, and he had no interest in dealing with another go-round anytime soon.

Nevertheless, there had been challengers. Thankfully, they'd been of the young, up-start type whose idea of planning was to strap on a gun and make a lot of noise. Between Chancy and Jack, as well as the two extra hands Travis had made available, most of the incidents had been dealt with in at least a moderately peaceful manner. Chancy still drew his gun much more often than he would've preferred, but never in a situation even slightly close to what they'd all dealt with at the shack.

After locking up another outlaw a kid, Chancy thought with barely a beard, Jack was coming in the office door as Chancy was preparing to head back out.

"What's this one been up to?" Jack gestured with his chin toward the hall with the cells. They'd stayed consistently full lately. Not to the bursting capacity they'd dealt with before, and none of the prisoners were whirling in and out with the speed McFarland's bail money had allowed, but some nights it was a tight squeeze.

"Mostly drinking," Chancy said. "By the smell of him, anyway. Caught him out in front of the Horseshoe trying to draw down on some fool over cards. Up to me, I'd have everybody bring their deck in and have us a little bonfire. Things cause more trouble than they're worth."

Jack smiled. "That includes the deck in your drawer there?"

Chancy smiled. "You won't believe this, but one time I played a hand of solitaire in here. Almost got done, too."

Jack laughed. "Cards are like guns, my friend. Sitting on a table they can't hurt nobody, but that sure don't mean everybody oughtta pick 'em up." He sat down in the extra chair in the office. "So, you just letting him sweat it out back there?"

Chancy perched on the corner of the desk. "I ain't never seen him before. Probably just another one passing through. I figure I'll let him stew for a bit. Kid can't be a day over eighteen. Maybe put a little fear in him and then ride him out to the edge of town and send him on his way. Oughtta make the point."

"Yeah," Jack mused.

"What's on your mind?"

"You been seeing a lot of unfamiliar faces lately?"

Chancy took off his hat and ran a hand through his hair. "Yeah, more'n usual, I'd say. You too, I take it."

Jack shrugged and shifted in his seat a little. "Well, where I been called out, I didn't think much of it at first. That stagecoach runs up north… Shoot, we've just been lucky we don't have to always deal with that as much as we have been. I've never been a fan of how they laid that one out, dead between the two towns. Makes it too easy for knocking 'em over when nobody knows for sure which jurisdiction they're passing through.

"Then the outskirts, well, I suppose that's part of the deal you make out yonder like that. You get the land, you get away from town some, but you also leave yourself a fair shake from help when somebody comes knocking in the middle of the night.

"I do my best to keep an eye on things, but the more this town spreads out, the more options boys like him"—he nodded toward the cells—"have for making a go of it. An empty wallet and an empty stomach can be motivating to a fella, just not always in the best way."

"What's your take?" Chancy asked, already guessing the answer.

"Well," Jack said, "much as I hate to say it, I'd guess now that ole Frank's been moved out, folks're seeing us as a bit of an opportunity."

"No one's running the show, so somebody needs to step up?"

Jack nodded. "Well, you gotta give him that. Long as Frank was in town, wasn't nobody willing to risk going up against him. Join him maybe, but the little wet-behind-the-ears ones like these fellas we been seein' lately would've moved right along. Snakes keep the rats at bay, so to speak."

"You saying we need another snake?" Chancy laughed.

"Cats do just as well." Jack grinned.

"Well..." Chancy stood up. "You saw what I did with Mr. Nichols. Seems to me we've got us a whole barnyard fulla cats out there."

Jack nodded. "Very true. But they've got other jobs to do besides mousin'."

"Just keep your eyes open," Chancy said. "I ain't saying you're wrong. In fact, from what I've been hearing, I reckon you hit the nail on the head. Time being though, I don't see much we can do but run around putting out the fires and see what happens next."

Just then, Jimmy Clark, out of breath, disheveled, and far from the counter at the apothecary where he usually stood, burst through the door. A strong smell of smoke came with him. "They're trying to burn it down!" the man cried without prelude. "I refused to give them the money, and they lit it on fire!"

Jack hopped up and patted Chancy on the shoulder as he raced out the door after the man. "Careful what you wish for, boss."

***

In a haberdashery on the south side of town, Harman Swally stood with two of his men, watching the apothecary across the street burn. None of the three had been involved in lighting the fire. At least not physically.

That task had been easily taken care of, with only a few dollars in the hands of an aimless youth passing through town. Over his years as an outlaw, Harm had learned the value of cheap labor and the motivation found in a pair of greenbacks.

For drifters like the boy, the crime was nothing more than drinking money, followed by a night in a bed and a few guaranteed meals.

Or at least that's how Harm sold the idea. What happened to the boy afterward was none of his concern. If the youth had any sense, he'd be far down the road in the opposite direction already. What Harm wanted to see, though, was what happened.

Across the street, the tailor and shop owner were working away in the bucket brigade, tossing water on the flames as the tin pails moved back and forth on the line between the apothecary and the closest water trough. The townsfolk had swarmed like flies when the chemist had come running out, and Swally couldn't blame them.

Crammed together like the buildings were, one man's fire could make short work of everyone's business. The boy was supposed to wait until Harm and his men had made it a little further away, but the unexpected exit of the haberdasher had given the three outlaws a fine view of the proceedings.

"Here they come," the man on his right, Mitchell, said.

Tearing down the main road in a cloud of dust, the sheriff and one of his deputies reined in their horses in front of the burning building, dismounting at a run.

"They're fast," Harm said, looking at his pocket watch.

"It ain't too far," Mitchell spoke again. Having spent some time in the town as a youth, he was the only one with some inside knowledge of the layout and goings-on. An older aunt still lived on the outskirts and treated Mitchell like she believed him to be an upstanding citizen. "Feller musta caught 'em both in the office. Ain't no other way they coulda got here so fast."

"Well, whatever the case," the other man said, "they got here. That's what we gotta keep in mind. Worst-case scenario, they're fast. And the way them boys look, even one of 'em is more than we wanna deal with."

"One of them is precisely what we want to deal with," Harm said. He turned to Mitchell. "The one on the right, correct?"

"Yep." Mitchell spat on the floorboards. "That's your man. Or at least that's what I'm guessin'. Tall feller, fast as sin with a gun. Don't take much lip from anybody. Auntie just adores him. Says he's the best sheriff they ever had."

"Well," Harm said. "I hope they didn't get used to it." He turned away from the window, wandering through the store to find the back exit of the building.

***

Two hours later, Harm Swally sat across from a very proper-looking woman. Her dark hair was up, ringlets framing either side of her lightly powdered face. She was behind a large oak desk, while he was on the other side in a velvet chair.

The room was sparse but elegant nonetheless. The woman had been even more sparing with her words. A note had been passed to Mitchell in the saloon with instructions to take it directly to Harm.

Ordinarily, the man would've balked at taking orders from anyone other than Swally, but this note had come from a tall blonde woman, Harm's favorite kind. If Swally had seen her, he would've recognized her as the woman in the blue dress who had escorted him into the office, ignoring his remarks and promptly exiting after he'd been seated.

The brunette across from him looked calmly across the desk, and for the first time in a long time, Swally felt uncomfortable. It's like she could read him, as if she were assessing him the way a man would a horse or a thief would a safe. She was looking for his flaws, his weaknesses. And Swally had the off-putting feeling she was accurately discovering each one.

Finally, after what felt like half an hour, she spoke. "You think this is a man's office, don't you?" she said.

Surprised, not just at her correct guess but at the audacity to say it, Harm was unsure how to respond.

"It's fine," the woman said. "I suppose it probably was, given the way things run out here. But I'll tell you something, Harm… may I call you Harm?"

He started to answer, but the woman continued speaking, the question more a sign of upbringing than a request for permission.

"I don't particularly care what you think about nearly anything. In fact, I don't particularly care what most people think. If you choose to wander about with the ignorant impression a man could do a better job, well, I suppose that is certainly your God-given right. Because you know what happens at the end of the day, Harm? Do you know how your ideals impact my life?"

The man shrugged. He was more than uncomfortable with this woman speaking to him in such a way.

"The answer, my dear sir, is that they don't impact me at all. Not one bit." She paused, looking at him. "What does impact me are your actions. That's why you're here today."

Swally folded his arms, looking over at her. "I don't know what you're getting at, lady, but I ain't—"

The woman waved her hand, cutting him off. "Save it, please. I'm not a judge, jury, or executioner. Well…" She smiled at him. "Not directly. From this point forward, it would behoove you to just assume I already know everything about you."

"Yeah?" Her arrogance was getting under his skin. "And how's that?"

"Well, take your friend Mr. Mitchell, for example," the woman said. "Sure, he's loyal. You can trust him to a certain extent. But he talks, does he not? Maybe not too often or too much, but a word will slip here or there."

"That rat bastard…"

The woman chuckled. "No, no, Mr. Swally. No need for that type of reaction. Mitchell hasn't been to see me. I simply use him to make my point. Men talk. Word spreads. It's the way life works. You can be angry about it, or you can use it to your advantage. I choose the latter. So, allow me to say this again: you would do best to assume I know everything about you. What we are doing here today is giving you a chance to know a little about me. Most importantly, that I'm someone very beneficial for you to know and someone very detrimental for you to cross."

Harm shrugged. *Fine,* he thought, *let the woman play her game.*

"Hm." She smiled, cupping her chin in a hand. "You're going to have to get used to it sooner or later, Harm. I'd suggest sooner. And here is your chance to show your willingness to cooperate and extend a hand of friendship. What are you doing in my town?"

"Your town?" he scoffed. "Last I heard, ain't nobody running this show."

"Ah, you see, word spreads. This word is one I've kept to myself, however. I've been biding my time, as they say. I assure you, though, this is simply a matter of planning. So, I'll ask again, and only once more, why are you here, Mr. Swally? And please don't waste my time with lies."

Harm shifted in his seat, trying to hold the woman's gaze but finding something too penetrating in her eyes. Whether or not he wanted to, he felt like he had to tell her the truth. Whatever was going on in her mind was hidden to him, but he had the distinct feeling it was cold and calculating. No more heart in her than in a wagon wheel or a blacksmith's hammer. "I'm here for the sheriff," he said finally.

"That's a fine start," the woman said. "Chancy Rosman has certainly made quite a splash since he made his appearance here. But surely you must have some reason. A vendetta, perhaps?"

"Look," Swally was losing his patience, and his discomfort only brought out his anger. "You say you got all the answers? What'm I even sittin' here for? You know who I am, then you know why I'm here. That good-for-nothin' shot my brother dead three years ago, and I intend to make that right."

"Ah." The woman leaned back in her chair, her fingers steepled in front of her and a smile on her face. "I like the fire in your eyes. I can do something with that."

Chapter 3
Travis' Plan

Ever since Teresa's abduction and the showdown at Blind Bluff, Chancy and Mayor Travis had been close. Travis had never admitted fully to what all he may or may not have done in assisting to bring down the outlaw Daniel Reese, and Chancy respected him more for it.

Talk was cheap in the west, after all. A man who could act and not need to parade it about town afterward was saying much more than most. So, when Chancy walked into the sheriff's station a few mornings later to see Travis already waiting in the chair across the desk, he wasn't overly concerned, though he was mildly surprised.

"First meeting of the day, huh?" Chancy smiled, hanging his hat on a peg behind the desk and then taking a seat behind the desk. "Don't suppose you just came by to reminisce?"

Travis smiled slightly. "I suppose you could call it that. You've been doing excellent work here, Chancy. And I don't just mean with Frank and his crew. The town has been different since you've been here. It's more settled. More at peace with itself, I suppose."

"Well, that's the way I prefer it," Chancy said. "I know I'm here to keep the order and all, but I don't mind saying it's a lot easier when everybody's on the same side."

"Almost everybody."

Chancy nodded. "There'll always be a few, I reckon."

"A few, yes, but as I'm sure you've noticed, the few are becoming more numerous as the days go by."

"Yeah," Chancy sighed. "Yeah, me and Jack was just discussing this t'other day. Shoot, even Teresa was giving me her predictions not too long ago. Is it safe to say you're of the same opinion with these things?"

"Without knowing exactly what 'these things' are, I don't wanna say one way or the other. But if your things have to do with the way this town's run in the past, I'd say Teresa and Jack are two people in the position to know. This is a delicate time for us. Uncertainty like this always is."

Chancy looked at the man for a moment. "It almost sounds like you're wishing there was a new Frank in town."

The mayor smiled grimly, crossing one leg over the other. "Not precisely that, no. But I, personally, and many of the townsfolk here, we've become accustomed to having problems and being able to both identify and solve them. As odd as it sounds, the feeling of not knowing can sometimes be more frustrating. We tend to gear up here, prepare for the worst. When there is no worst, no tangible thing we are working against, the idleness becomes its own problem."

"I'd say that's your problem right there, then," Chancy said, leaning back in his chair.

"Yes," Travis said. "That's been my conclusion as well. Nature always has something to throw at us, be it too much rain, too little rain. The storms that whip up out of nowhere. Sick livestock. Poor harvests. But these things are part of the life. We're prepared for those. What one can't prepare for is the unknown."

Chancy thought quietly, then leaned forward, folding his hands on the desktop. "Let's not let our folks be idle then. You talk like all these people are good at is solving a problem once it's started. And from what I've seen, you're not wrong. At least not entirely. But you know what happened in here the night we was waitin' to send off McFarland. Nichols and his boys were ready. They were darn near eager to take a part in watching out for this town."

"McFarland was a real problem, though. The men outside your door were tangible, visible."

"But didn't nobody know they were gonna be here?"

"True. Outside of deputizing the entire town, though, I'm not sure how we can expect to have watchdogs at every corner. What happened on the night you're referring to was mostly luck. Bravery and strong morals of course, but luck that Nichols was where he was when he was."

"And what I'm saying is I bet that don't make a lot of difference. Nichols, sure, he's a little more fired up than most, but he's no mule among the horses. Way I figure, if it hadn't been Nichols, it would've been someone else."

"You have a lot of faith in these folks. I'm not saying it's ungrounded, but that's a new perspective for you, Sheriff."

"Oh, I'll be the first to admit it's new. You know as well as I do, two months ago I'd've taken on any problem by my lonesome and preferred it that way. But it's foolish to not take advantage of resources when they're sittin' there."

"And that's how you see the town? Resources?"

"Look," Chancy said. "All I know is when I asked Andy Nichols to keep his eye out, maybe it wasn't the best idea. But thankfully, it worked out in the end. Now, if a boy could show that much backbone, be that valuable, imagine if we had the whole town keeping an eye out."

Travis smiled. "Chancy, I'm glad to hear you say that. I've had some talk about whether you'd be on board with even the idea of receiving what we could perceive as help, but it looks like you've concluded that on your own."

Chancy leaned his head to one side. "That was your whole point to begin with, wasn't it?"

The mayor laughed. "You make it sound like I'm a confidence man. I simply had an idea and wanted to let you think it through for yourself."

"And if I'd disagreed?"

Travis stood up. "I guess we'll never know. There's a meeting at the church this evening. Quite a few folks are going to be there, and it would be very useful to us if we had our sheriff in attendance."

"Ah…" Chancy grinned. "And that's why Jack was insisting he'd work tonight. You're slick, Travis. I gotta give you that."

The mayor reached over to shake Chancy's hand and then headed for the door. "Slick, maybe. Careful, always. I'll look forward to seeing you this evening, sir."

"Yeah." Chancy shook his head, smiling. "You too."

***

That evening, after a lengthy (if rather mundane, Chancy thought) speech by the mayor and a few local concerned citizens, the sanctuary of the Methodist church had been turned over to the people for a question-and-answer session, putting the sheriff, his deputies, and the rest of the town council up for what felt like all questions regarding the mayor's new plan.

Mostly, things had gone as Chancy expected. The room, built to house what had originally been a small band of settlers, had been expanded and renovated over the years but still was at a standing-room-only capacity.

The business owners had come to ensure they were fairly represented. The workingmen had committed to a late night so as not to be left out of the discussion. Those with wives had brought them, those with children likewise. Even Teresa had a small band of single women around her off to one side.

While the questions quickly turned to scenarios that were highly unlikely or highly specific or both. After about thirty minutes, though, James Nichols, apparently taking the role of unofficial leader of the citizen's, was settled the crowd and got down to generalized specifics.

"Do we need to take watches?" he asked. "Come up with some kind of schedule? I can post things in the shop. Most folks are in there at least once a week. Keep everybody in the know that way, make sure folks know where they need to be and when."

"No, no," the mayor said, giving Chancy an exasperated though rather pleased smile, "as I've mentioned many times, this is not an official, government-sponsored situation we're dealing with. And I'd like to take this time to reiterate, yet again, that it is in your best interests to keep that at the forefront of your minds. The laws here aren't changing. If you discharge a weapon, we will hold you responsible for it."

"Well, what about when they was comin' for Frank?" a voice called out.

James Nichols hopped up again. "Hey, I was protecting the peace!"

"Under whose authority?" another voice yelled.

"Folks!" the mayor cut in. "We aren't here to get into specifics. As we've seen in the instance of Mr. Clark and the chemicals in his shop, some things are going to have to be dealt with on a case-by-case basis. What we're trying to discuss tonight are generalities. Codes of conduct."

Chancy made a gesture toward Travis and then stood up. "Look, we can spend all night here talking about who can do what and when and where they can do it. That ain't gonna get us too far, though. Lord knows most of the answers I give about them chemicals was just made up, anyway." He grinned, and even Jimmy Clark smiled a bit. "But all me and the mayor is askin' of you is to keep doing what you're doin' but be confident about it. It ain't no secret me and Teresa there spend most nights sitting out on the porch at the boarding house, and despite what some of you may think..." He looked at one older woman, who blushed. "It ain't because we're planning a wedding."

"Not yet!" the jokester called out again.

Chancy blushed just slightly, though he hoped they could take it for a flush in his cheeks. Packed beyond capacity, the room had grown hot, stale.

"The fact is," he said, pressing the air in front of him to restore some order, "we talk about the town. We talk about what we seen that day, what we done. What we got on our minds. I'd just about bet you folks have the same conversations at your own dinner tables, or your own porches, or your own pump handles, or wherever. I ain't got no problem with that, and there ain't no law against it.

"The only problem is while the preacher'll tell ya gossip spreads like wildfire, it don't always spread where it needs to. Or half the time, what finally makes it to my ears is as far from the truth as we are from New York. So what I'm sayin' is keep your eyes open. Keep your ears open." He scanned the crowd for a moment. "Now I don't see him in here tonight, but a good many of you know Andy Nichols done as much to save my hide as most folks here. And all he did was listen, pay attention, and let me know when something important was going on."

"Yeah, and he took a bullet for it," someone muttered.

Chancy tried to pinpoint where the voice had come from but, after a moment, realized the source didn't matter so much as the sentiment.

"You're right," Chancy said. "And that's why we ain't here tellin' you any of y'all have to do nothing. I like to think we got us a town of men here that'll make sure we ain't gotta rely on our children and womenfolk to stay safe, but I'd be lying if I say I didn't trust them children and womenfolk with my life. I do it every time I walk down the streets out here, every time I climb in that saddle. You don't wanna be a part of that, well, all right. That's your choice in the matter.

"But if somebody else does, that's their choice, and you folks that wanna hunker down and keep to yourselves, you go right ahead. Long as you ain't a part of the problem, you ain't got no problem with me. Or anybody else. I'll make sure of that."

A wave of murmurs and mutters passed through the crowd. Small discussions that seemed on the verge of becoming arguments poked their heads up.

Mayor Travis stood again, though not to take Chancy's place, the sheriff realized. It was to show solidarity. "Before we finish up for tonight," Travis said, "I'm sure there are still some of you who want more solid information. You want steps to follow. After all, that is something we excel at here. I was just telling Chancy this morning; we are a town that sees its problems and then solves its problems. So, you're probably wondering, how do we solve a problem we can't see?

"Quite simple. You are all smart folks." A small titter came from the crowd, a few jesters throwing out names. Travis waited for silence. "You all have your lives and jobs and businesses to attend to. The most important thing we, as a town, can do is to keep these things up. What good will a perfectly safe town be if we have no medicine from Mr. Clark? No meal from Mr. Nichols? We would secure ourselves into starvation.

"The only change I'm encouraging here is that you be aware of those around you. Know your neighbors. We're all aware that with the stage run near to here, we get our fair share of strangers. And that's good. I'm not telling you to buy them dinner or give them a bed in your home. But neither am I telling you to come running every time you see a new face. Simply be yourselves. Be cordial. Strike up a conversation. Don't forget that we are the prime example of the general goodness of people. We've got a church bursting with folks here tonight simply because you all want to make sure that we all stay safe.

"Now, to address issues that may come up, I've implemented two new positions in town. One will be in my office. The other will be at Sheriff Rosman's office. Should you have a concern, or information that you feel is important for us to know, please come to one of these places and inform the appropriate person. As the sheriff noted, often you will know things long before we do. Other than having the chance to say told ya so, that doesn't help the town too terribly much.

"So, please..." The mayor looked across the crowd at those sitting in the front with him. "Be aware, be responsible, and look out for one another. Thank you." Travis turned to those behind him, gesturing toward a side door.

Outside, Chancy stood with the small group of men chosen to represent the town and its safety that evening. "Went about as well as you could hope, I imagine," he said to Travis when the man emerged.

"Yes, I thought so as well." The mayor glanced at the small group of men. "That may or may not make much difference in town, though. If I were to guess, we will be overwhelmed for a few days with information about whose cat is drinking out of whose saucer, but that can't be avoided. Most of you are aware of names to listen for, incidents to pay attention to. I can't speak for Chancy, but I assure you that my door is always open to anyone standing here right now. Don't hesitate, no matter how trivial you think something might be."

The men nodded, and a few yawned. The news was anything but new, though having it reiterated boosted morale, if only slightly.

"Why don't you all head home for the night as well," Travis said. "The last thing we need is a meeting after the meeting. We'll be here until the sun comes up."

They exchanged a few handshakes and muttered pleasantries before Chancy felt the mayor tug at his sleeve. He turned back, eyebrows up.

"There's one more thing I wanted to talk to you about, but I didn't want to say so in front of the others. Picking favorites is bad in my position but picking enemies can be even worse. I haven't mentioned this to you previously because I had no reason to but given the slew of information we just encouraged the townsfolk to give us, there's a good chance a name is going to come up you'll need to know."

Chancy put his hands in his pockets. "Can't be so bad or I think I'd've heard it by now."

"Yes." The mayor looked off into the distance. "It's a tricky situation. You're familiar with the Horseshoe, of course. And Addie's. And most places in town, I suppose. I wonder though, have you ever been out to the Shipyard?"

Chancy couldn't help but grin. The Shipyard was a saloon so perfectly on the edge of town that there were rumors it wasn't even part of Elkhorn proper. Granted, Chancy always assumed most of those had been started by the owner himself, who did little to calm the concerns of those who thought of it as a tough place.

"I was out that way a time or two," Chancy said. "Not really my kinda joint, but you go where the job takes you sometimes."

"Yes, that's about what I'd assumed," Travis said. "Here's the thing: the man who owns it, Shipman Buchanon..."

"That's his real name? I figured it was just what folks call him."

"Yes," Travis said. "Sailing family, somehow, or so he claims. But Ship is, well, he's a tricky one. There are always plenty of rumors about what goes on out there, but for the life of me, I've never been able to see that they are anything more than just rumors."

Chancy nodded. "So, it'll come up."

"Probably a lot," Travis said. "So, take it with a grain of salt, but don't write it off entirely. My gut tells me something's going on there."

"It just ain't telling you what or with who."

"Precisely."

The sheriff smiled a bit. "This wouldn't be the main reason for this new program you're starting up, would it?"

Travis patted Chancy on the shoulder. "Entirely? No, of course not. But if word spreads..." He shrugged. "Have a good night, Chancy."

"You too, Mayor."

Chapter 4
What Happened to Carl Renfrew?

Ship Buchanon's name came up frequently in the ensuing week, which was not something Ship had either counted on or appreciated. While his relationship with the law had been tenuous for most of his life, and the saloon often felt more like a hideout for passing guns than a respectable business, he had done his best to keep things under control.

Before Chancy Rosman had become sheriff, there had always been a kind of understanding between Ship and the regulators. He kept to his end of town, solved his own problems, and, mostly, stayed out of sight.

It hadn't hurt that, for a good chunk of time, Frank McFarland's men had reveled in spending their off hours in the dark saloon. While they often found themselves in the Horseshoe, those on the other side of the law always headed to the Shipyard. Though one couldn't precisely let one's guard down in the place, there was a fragile truce understood to be held around the building.

Partly this was because of the lack of other saloons allowing such boisterous clientele. The other part was that

Ship kept his side of the deal with the former sheriff. Problems were solved by Ship swiftly and with finality. His word was the closest thing to law once a man wandered into his end of town.

And that had been fine. For a time. The more clean-cut residents kept to their part of town and Ship kept to his. On the very rare occasion Ship had needed to deal with the local lawmen, they had done it through an arranged meeting on neutral ground.

Before Chancy, these meetings could've meant many things, and it wasn't unheard of that Ship's help was requested in taking care of problems the sheriff couldn't handle in the most legal of ways.

Because of this back-scratching arrangement, Ship Buchanon had expected to continue spending his days out of the eye of the law, even after McFarland's man had got himself shot.

What he hadn't bet on was Rosman coming in and throwing off the balance of things. Sure, Chancy hadn't been down to the saloon much, and he hadn't caused Ship any problems yet. At least not any of account.

McFarland being scooped by the marshals, was bound to happen eventually. Buchanon had been around long enough to know that men like him either made their money and disappeared or were run off. The business savvy of Frank had been nice, though.

The thing that really got under Ship's skin, though, was the rumors he'd been hearing from some of his more trusted patrons. While there had been a small increase in customers over the last two weeks, most of it had been early on. It was curious, but not unheard of.

Every now and again, a group of upstarts would get it in their heads they had what it took to be a part of the gang out at the Shipyard. Most times it was harmless, and they realized fast enough they were in over their heads. On the rare occasion that wasn't the case, either some other posse ran them off within a few days, or even more rarely, the fresh faces showed they had what it took to hang around.

What bothered Ship about the new faces he'd been seeing wasn't their youth or their false bravado. It was that they clearly were there for only one reason, and it was to talk.

Shooting the breeze was fine, and there were plenty of jobs that had been planned in the dark corners of the Shipyard. But too many questions from new folks was one of the few things that could really cause Ship problems.

If word got around that a gunslinger couldn't speak too freely in the Shipyard, they would desert the place in no time. Even Buchanon himself preferred to stay out of the loop for the most part. The less a man knew, the less they could beat out of him.

This evening, Ship was sitting on one of his own chairs at the end of the bar. His cousin had come in earlier that evening, beckoning the owner down to the empty seat.

Willet wasn't always reliable, wasn't always honest in fact, but when things really came down to it, he was family, and Ship knew the fellow put family first. So, when Willet started discussing the very things that had been bothering Ship, the bar owner knew the info was probably good.

"It's something between the mayor and the sheriff," Willet was saying. "Trying to turn the whole town against us, if you ask me."

Ship stroked the stubble on his chin. Willet's constant use of "us" and "we" and "our" could be tedious. Only one man owned the Shipyard, and that man was the only one responsible for it. But given the situation at hand, Ship let the phrasing slide for the time being. "That'd account for what I been seein'," he said.

"That's what I thought, too," Willet said, excited at his cousin's agreement. "Been too many unfamiliar faces in here for it to just be a coincidence. Asides that, they ain't even half of 'em new faces. Hell, folks I been seein' coming in and outta here, they been around well long enough to know this ain't their place to be."

Ship knew Willet was right. He just hadn't wanted to believe the town could turn so fully. Sure, Frank had swayed most folks, but that had been different. A fellow signed up with Frank McFarland because he thought he was getting something out of it.

A fellow signed up to be a snitch for the sheriff, well, where was the payoff? He leaned on the bar and looked at his cousin.

"Well, what do ya s'pose is causing 'em to do that, Willet? We ain't been doing nothing here we ain't been doing for years."

Willet leaned forward, mirroring the posture. "What I hear is they's wanting to clean up the town."

Ship laughed, leaning back in his chair. "Hell, this town's clean enough. What're they wanting, to eat out of the water troughs and turn all their guns in? Town like this needs people like us. We keep it in balance. Last sheriff understood that."

"I know, Ship. Oh, I know." Willet leaned back as well, earning an irritated gaze from Shipman. "But this new feller, he ain't like the old one. This guy, well…" The man tried to come up with his words carefully, hoping to impress his cousin. "He's got mortals."

"Morals?"

"Yeah. He's got morals."

Ship sighed. "Well, that's about the worst kinda sheriff we could have." He took a long drink from a mug of beer in front of him. "So, they're gonna clean up the town by running us out?"

Willet nodded noncommittally. "Now with that, I ain't real sure. That's the thing, Ship, ain't no names. Ain't no wanted posters. It's like they're just taking everybody to task."

"Hm," Ship muttered. "Makes it awfully hard to hit a target when you don't know what it is."

"Well, I think that's the plan though, see? They just gather up any bit of news they can find out about anybody, and then they go after 'im. Could be you, could never be you. Ain't no sense in it."

"Now there you've got a point," Ship said. "There ain't no sense in coming out here after me. I run this business just like any other fella runs one. Take care of the people in this town the way they need to be taken care of."

"I just hope they see it that way," Willet said. "Cause right now, it seems like it don't matter who ya are. If somebody drops your name, them boys'll be huntin' ya down."

"Sounds like we need to make sure my name stays out of things, then." Ship gave Willet a meaningful look.

"Hey!" Willet held his hands up. "I don't say nothin' to nobody but you. You know that. We're family."

"That's true," Ship said, trying to not run through the list of times he'd pulled Willet's bacon out of the fire. "Well," he said finally, "you keep doing what you're doing. I 'preciate you keeping me in the know."

Willet smiled. "We're family," he said again.

"All right," Ship said, "get outta here. I got a bar to run, and you got folks to listen to."

Willet tossed back a shot of whiskey Ship had poured for him out of a bottle on the bar. "You got it."

***

While Ship knew Willet could only be relied on to a certain extent, the man would eventually come back with some news. The only troublesome part was sorting through it to figure out what was useful and what was rumor. At the same time, though, Ship figured he'd rather have too much information in his situation than not enough.

Double-crosses were so common in his typical run-ins that both parties had begun to assume the approach was part of the deal. What Ship hadn't counted on was Willet coming in the very next night, hot under the collar and practically dragging him to the back room.

"Calm down," Ship grunted, pushing Willet back lightly and trying to get some space between them. "The place ain't on fire, and I ain't heard no gunshots. What's got you all riled?"

"You told me to pay attention, Ship, and I did," the man said, breathing hard. "There's one feller been doing an awful lot of the talking, too. You know Renfrew? From out on the north-side?"

Ship thought for a moment, running through the faces in his mind. For a man who rarely left his neighborhood, he had an incredible knack for remembering both names and faces. This particular talent was one that had saved his hide more than once, and it sounded like it was about to again. "Carl Renfrew?" he asked.

Willet nodded. "That's the one. 'Parently he's been trying to make a name for hisself some which way. Folks say he's trying to impress a gal, but—"

Ship held up a hand. "Kid his age ain't got no good reason for anything," he said. "He even shaving yet?"

"Oh sure, Ship. He's twenty, twenty-five these days. Took over the farm when his daddy died a year or two back."

"That's right," Ship said, looking up at the ceiling. "I recall hearing something about that now." After a moment, he looked back at Willet, a frown on his face. "So, Carl's looking to move up in the world, is he? Got the land and now he's looking for the lady? I suppose that's got something to do with me then."

"Well, it's like you said," Willet responded. "There ain't no real payoff for these townsfolk, far as I can see. But I reckon Renfrew figures he can still get something out of it, even if it ain't money."

"And what, exactly, is it?"

"Word is he's been spouting off about this place. Now I don't know if he's after you, specifically, or just anybody he can nab, but he hasn't been making it no secret. He's wanting to turn this place inside out."

Shipman laughed, folding his arms across his chest. "Boy's a damn fool."

"Yeah, yeah," Willet said. "That may very well be. Fact he'd 'bout *have* to be if he's thinking he can rat out anybody in here and not have problems. But thing is, it ain't stopping him none. He's on his way down here now."

"I see." Ship stroked his chin. "You're sure of this?"

"Sure as I can be," Willet said. "I heard him at the Horseshoe saying this was his next stop, so I cut out to find you first."

"That's good work, Willet." Shipman patted him on the shoulder.

"So what's the plan, then?"

"Ah, you let me handle that part. You done good. Go pour yourself a drink."

"Sure thing, boss." Willet lit up. Either at the compliment or the free booze, Ship wasn't sure which.

Following his cousin back out to the barroom, Shipman gestured over Willet's shoulder to a table of men off to one side, playing a hand of cards with little interest. At the signal, all three mucked their cards and walked over to the barman. The Shipyard wasn't safe for everyone. That was accepted, but these three clearly had no qualms about leaving their greenbacks and coins on the table for the moment.

"What's the word, boss?" one asked as the quartet huddled in the small space between the bar and the backroom.

"Word is we got a rat comin' in tonight," Ship said. "Y'all know Carl Renfrew?"

A few puzzled looks were his only answer.

"Ain't no difference," Ship said. "Look, you just go back to your game like you was, but when you get the nod from me, you pay special attention to the man I'm talkin' to. I think he may need to be talkin' with you all, as well."

The first man grinned, showing a gold tooth. "How much talking you wanting us to do?"

Ship thought for a moment. "Enough to make sure he don't come back," he said. "But enough that he can spread the word rats ain't welcome."

"You got it, boss."

Without need or request for further instruction, the three men moved back to their table while Ship took his place behind the bar.

Willet slid down the wood to sit across from him. "I was thinkin'," Willet said. "Seein' as how I's the one who helped you out with all this, how 'bout you let me follow it through?"

Ship raised his eyebrows. "To the end?"

"Whatever you got them boys doin', I can do just as well."

"Y'know, part of what makes this work is us keeping our hands clean," Ship said.

Willet shrugged. "Sometimes, yeah."

Shipman looked at him. Willet had always been a good pair of ears but usually shied away from anything that had the slightest hint of violence to it. "You know what they're planning to do?" he asked.

Willet squared his shoulders and tried to puff out his chest. "I know, Ship. And I ain't the smartest guy in the world. I know that too. But another thing I know is you keep me outta things. Now maybe that's cause we're family, but I been around a long time. I ain't no kid. If I'm gonna be here, I wanna be pulling my weight."

Ship thought for a moment. "All right," he said. "But you follow Charlie's lead."

Willet glanced over at the table, noting the man with the gold tooth. "Okay, will do."

A few minutes later, the batwing doors swung open, and the sauntering form of Carl Renfrew entered the saloon. Ship couldn't be sure, but it looked like the boy had tried to dirty himself up some, tried to make himself blend in with what he assumed the rougher crowd would look like.

Instead, he looked precisely like what he was: a young man with too much confidence in a place that only gave respect to those who'd earned it.

Renfrew walked straight up to the bar, his chest out and a smug grin on his face. "Whiskey," he said, patting the wood.

Ship looked at him for a minute, catching Charlie's eye over the youth's shoulder. "You sure this is the place you wanna be drinkin'?" Ship asked, knowing he'd never convince Renfrew to leave but wanting to say he'd tried, should he ever be asked.

"One place's good as another," Carl said. "I reckon."

"You reckon?" Ship sighed. "Guess I can't argue with that."

"Reckon not," Carl said, laughing alone at his own joke.

As Ship reached for the bottle, he nodded slightly to Charlie, and the men rose as a group, moving up to the bar quietly, one on either side of Renfrew and the third behind him. Willet, seeing the plan begin, left his seat, and joined the posse.

"What's this all about?" Carl said, his smile instantly gone as the men leaned down on either side of him. His bluster, and much of the color in his face, vanished with it.

"We's just wanting to have us a little chat," Charlie said, smiling to flash his gold tooth. "You all right with that, Ship?"

Buchanon smiled, slid the shot glass to the youth, and nodded. "You're gonna want that."

Carl's hand shook as he downed the shot. "Well," he said, looking between the men. "Let's talk."

"No, no," Charlie said. "This here's too public. Ship's got a fine office upstairs. Perfect place for doing business."

"Hey, I ain't got no business to attend to here," Carl said, too late realizing his words would make no difference, and likely very little with the girl he supposedly had his eye on.

"You're here now," Charlie said, boosting the young man off the barstool by the back of his shirt. "So, we're making it our business."

With a quick glance from Willet to Ship, which Ship answered with a nod, Carl Renfrew disappeared up the side stairs with the four men.

Ship gestured to an old man sitting in the corner and smoking a cigarette on his own. Without a word, the old-timer stepped over to an even older piano and banged out a tune, which, despite his best efforts, did very little to cover the yells and crashes coming from upstairs.

Only a few patrons had the lack of control to look up, even fewer had the gall to comment in whispered tones. Shipman merely stood behind the bar, whistling along tunelessly with the music, and wiping mugs with a dirty rag.

After about five minutes, the sounds from upstairs stopped momentarily, only to be followed by raised voices again. Ship's ears perked up. He knew he shouldn't have sent Willet up there. Whatever was going on was surely going to fall at his cousin's feet.

As if called for, the door at the top of the stairs burst open, and Willet came down the steps two at a time, stumbling and leaning on the handrail in his rush.

"It was an accident!" he cried out, running over to Shipman.

Close behind him came Charlie, his jaw clenched in anger.

Ship held up a hand to Willet and looked over at the man. "How bad?"

"Dead."

"Damn it, Willet!"

"I didn't mean to!" Willet cried. "I got carried away!"

Shipman grabbed his cousin by his collar, buttons popping off as the barman pulled him closer. "First off, shut your damn mouth. You come in here warning us about folks watching, then you come down screaming about a dead man? The hell's the matter with you?"

"I didn't…" Willet fought against his panic as he fought against Shipman's grasp. "I just—"

"Enough, I said," Shipman cut him off. He turned to Charlie. "You boys can take care of the body?"

Charlie nodded. "Yeah. We can handle that."

"Good." Shipman turned back to Willet. "As for you, you need to get lost. Now. Anything you been worrying about happening to me, you worry twice as much about it happening to you. We got an entire room full of people, seen you go up there with him and then come tearing out like your tail's on fire. Don't take a genius to piece it together. You get, and don't come back till I say so."

Willet looked like he was about to protest then, realizing he had no other options, grabbed a bottle of whiskey from the bar, took a slug, and wiped his mouth on his sleeve. "Thanks, Ship. I knew you'd come through."

"Get," Ship said. As Willet left, perhaps drawing even more attention than he had rushing down the stairs, Shipman turned back to Charlie. "Take the body out the back way. Probably best you boys lie low for a time, too."

"You got it, boss."

"Here," Shipman reached under the bar and pulled out a full bottle. "Keep you from getting thirsty."

Charlie nodded, grabbed the whiskey, and disappeared back up the stairs to the office.

Chapter 5
The Points of the Compass

Harm Swally tromped up the wooden steps to the upper office he'd not enjoyed visiting the first time and had gained no warm feelings for in the few times since.

The woman, Anne-Marie, was off-putting. Not that she was obnoxious or hard to look at, but she was quiet. She had a certain smugness about her Harm didn't like, a small grin he'd like to smack off her face.

The funny thing was, he thought, it wasn't the fact she was a woman that set his teeth on edge. It was the way she seemed to use it. Out here in the west, most women knew they had to use their femininity one way or another if they were going to make a go of it, either by roping in a solid, dependable man or by briefly roping in several a night.

This woman seemed to act as if she were above all that. It was the arrogance that got under Harm's skin.

He'd spent plenty of time working with the who's who and the who's that of the criminal world as he'd traveled around the Texas and Oklahoma territories, and he'd gotten to be a good judge of character, even if the standard type of character was bad. There were still variations from the norm.

Some fellows would shoot you just as soon as look at you. Those, oddly enough, were the kind Harm liked best. You knew where you stood with them. No questions, no tricky details to throw off a plan. No backstabbing.

Anne-Marie, though, he couldn't shake the feeling that every time he entered the office, she was about to spring something on him he hadn't been looking out for. Maybe he was just spooking himself, but his gut had kept him alive this long, so no sense in not trusting it now.

The big problem with Anne-Marie, it frustrated him to admit, was that even his gut was confused. She seemed on the up and up, talked like she knew what she was after, and sounded as if she'd been to a few rodeos herself. But she wasn't telling him everything. And that was another problem: everything about what?

She'd said to keep her in the loop, like he had any information she wouldn't get hours before. Whoever she was, however she was working, she had people all over.

If his gut hadn't said otherwise, he'd almost think she was playing him, trying to rope him into something before handing him over to the sheriff. But there was a roughness to her that, despite her fancy dresses and perfumes, still belied a street hustler and outlaw mind at work.

Harm walked in the room and sat down in the chair across from her at the desk. She looked poised, comfortable, and it immediately gave Harm a feeling of unease. That damn smile was there again. Her eyes watched him as he moved, as he sat. They darted down to his crossed legs, his jiggling boot.

With an effort, Harm forced himself to sit still. He might be uncomfortable—shoot, nervous even, if he were honest—but the lady probably already knew all that. No reason to give her more to feed off.

After a long silence, the purpose of which seemed to be no more or less than showing she was at ease with it, Harm spoke up. "Well, you called me in here. You got me now. What do ya want?"

"Not much of a one for pleasantries," Anne-Marie said, her eyes holding his gaze. "I suppose that can be admired in a man, at the right time."

"I don't see what we really got to chat about," Harm said. "You know why I'm here. You know what I'm planning on doing. Didn't seem to me you had much in the way of fondness for that sheriff, so I don't see as how we got much beef."

"Beef?" she smiled. "No, we certainly have no beef."

The simple repetition of the word set Harm's teeth on edge. It was a perfectly fine term, and yet when she threw it back at him like that, it sounded childish, silly. It made him feel talked down to. And that made him angry. "Then I reckon you's wasting my time." He went to stand up.

It was a small sound, barely noticeable over the scraping of the chair across the floor, but Harm heard the little snort of laughter as clear as a church bell. Instinctively, his hand went for his revolver, even in the midst of regretting it. Before he could draw, he felt a cold metal barrel pressed up against the back of his skull.

Damn, there are always two of them. Stupid for forgetting that.

"Perhaps we have more beef than I realized," Anne-Marie said. "Mercedes, if you could." She made a gesture, and Harm felt his gun being jerked from the holster, then the knife from his boot. "I didn't think I'd have to ask you to leave these at the desk," Anne-Marie continued, "but I see we may need to adapt our policies."

Behind him, Harm heard the other woman, Mercedes, pull the door closed. It was another thing that made his skin crawl. He heard the door close, but not the woman walking away. He hadn't even known she'd walked in, and yet she'd probably been standing behind him from the moment he sat down. Whatever happened with these ladies down the road, Harm would not have any easy go of it if they ended up on opposite sides of something.

"Please sit down," Anne-Marie said. "Perhaps we can try this again."

Harm let his weight fall into the chair, the closest he could come to a disrespectful gesture without going too far. For all he knew, the other woman had only closed the door and still stood with a gun pointed at him.

"She left," Anne-Marie said, as if reading his thoughts. "You can relax." She smiled. "At least a little."

Instead, Harm fidgeted, trying to hide his nerves behind nonchalant gestures, though with little success.

"Now," the woman continued. "You want to know why you're here. I think that's a fair question, and I'll answer that shortly. You want to know if I'm concerned about your plans for Sheriff Rosman. That we can discuss as well. But first I'd like to tell you a story. Do you like stories, Harm?"

The man grunted and shrugged a shoulder.

"I'm sorry, what was that?" the woman asked.

"I said sure," Harm grunted.

"Excellent," Anne-Marie said. "I think you'll find this one especially appealing, as it should be relatable to you."

She paused again, one of her pointless pauses that only grated on his nerves. Was he supposed to reply? What did a guy say to that? Just before he could speak up, she began again.

"Not so long ago, in this very town, there was a man of action. He was going to take things over, run the show, be the big man, as it were. He had the brilliant scheme that, if a man wanted to gain a following, he would do best by offering an incentive. One catches more flies with honey than with vinegar, as the saying goes.

"So, this man decided he would make offers the people couldn't refuse. Of course, they weren't the best of offers. But in the excitement of the moment, men will often sign away everything at the promise of more later. I'm sure you're familiar with gambling, given your background, Mr. Swally. Perhaps you've even fallen into a similar circumstance a time or two.

"Now I'm here to tell you that, while there are some brilliant men back east following a plan very much like this one, the man here was not so brilliant. He was smart, and he was ruthless, two things a fellow needs in Nebraska, I'm finding. But there was something else. He had a kind of arrogance about him. A complacency, to a certain extent. He was a man with big plans, but he'd been doing well for too long.

He believed the stories about himself. This man had grown so used to money solving his problems, either in many small amounts or grandiose chunks, that he stopped believing there was a problem money couldn't solve.

"And so, as you might've guessed, eventually, a problem money couldn't solve came along. There is a fundamental flaw in the theory of buying folks, Harm, and that is that everyone, from the pastor to the man cleaning the spittoons, loves it just as much as you do. Now, I'm sure you've got some response here, but allow me to stop you. Everyone loves money. I would never be so foolish to argue with you there.

But what our man forgot is that some people, many people, love other things as well. Things money can't buy. So when the offer you are making loses its appeal, well, you're not just in a pickle, you're in the barrel."

Harm ran a hand through his hair. He hadn't wanted to come here in the first place, and he certainly hadn't wanted to come and listen to some tired old story. "Can we get to the part that has to do with me?" he asked.

"Oh, this all has to do with you, Mr. Swally. Because the man who tried to buy everyone is now spending his time with the US Marshals, and we likely won't be seeing him again for quite a while. But that doesn't mean he isn't still useful to us. So, Harm, what can we learn from this man's mistakes?"

Harm sighed, looking up at the ceiling.

"Fine," Anne-Marie said. "I'll spare you the test. The answer, sir, is that goodwill only lasts for a moment. Those who benefited from this man were soon unhappy with their deals. They didn't want to honor the commitment they had willingly made before. And when that happened, all the work, all the time, all the hours our man had put into his peaceful yet thorough undertaking just… poof, blew away with the wind."

"Well, that's fine," Harm said. "But I ain't planning on no peaceful nothing. And I didn't come here for the town. I came here for the sheriff. Once I settle my score with him, you ain't got to worry about seeing me around no more."

The woman giggled again, doing nothing to hide her mirth. "Oh, Harm, I'm not worried about seeing you around now. But since you're here, why don't you let me tell you what we can do instead of trying to buy this town?"

"What's that?" Harm scoffed. "Burn it down?"

"There…" She smiled. "See? You can be quite bright occasionally. We're going to burn it down. Or more precisely, we're going to burn down roughly half of it. You see, Harm, what the man in our story miscalculated was not the amount of money. He didn't err when he bribed the sheriff or the saloonkeeper. Where he made his mistake was thinking that money was more powerful than fear. I've never made that mistake, sir. I intend to own this town in a way that puts my predecessor's brief foray to shame. And since you are here, and since our aims align at least somewhat, I'd like to offer you the opportunity to join me in some of the fun."

Harm looked down, shaking his head. "I told ya, I'm here for the sheriff. And that's it. You wanna burn the place down, you be my guest. But that ain't no concern of mine."

"Now, Harm, think about what you're saying for a moment. Who always comes when there's a fire?"

Harm sighed. "The sheriff."

"Exactly. And I'll be the first to tell you, the man they have as sheriff right now, he's fast, and he's smart. Though, I suppose you have some experience with his style. What I'm offering you here, though, is not just the sheriff at a burning building. I'm offering you the sheriff at any burning building you choose, when you choose, and with as many of your posse hanging about as you wish."

"An ambush that ain't exactly an ambush," Harm mused.

"Oh, it would be exactly an ambush," the woman laughed. "But not the kind he would expect. One building burning could be an accident, or it could be a scheme. He won't know and he'll be on his toes, as they say. Two buildings will make him wonder if this was a coincidence or the beginning of something. Five burned buildings, though. Not only will he know he's got a serious problem on his hands, but he'll be tired and scrambling to keep the peace among his own people."

"And he won't be expecting me, cause nothin' will have happened at the other'ns except the burning." Harm grinned.

"Now, you're understanding," Anne-Marie said. "So I'll make my offer again. Would you like to assist me in my goals if the payment is your goal?"

Harm looked up at the woman, for once feeling confident. "You just hand me the matches."

***

About a week later, Chancy was walking around a dry goods store on the east side of town as the wooden frame smoldered and a handful of small fires burned themselves out. A dozen men still lingered, discussing what happened, what they could've done better.

The folks in Elkhorn were better organized than he'd seen in a lot of places. They at least tried to have organization, as opposed to the free-for-all of volunteers he'd seen in other towns. Often, that kind of setup led to the fire burning until it put itself out, though there would be no lack of people standing around watching it. Thankfully, here, the men were forming a plan.

And given that this was the third fire in roughly six days, they were going to need it.

Chancy picked up a few buckets from the ground, carrying them over to a wagon and tossing them in the back just as Mayor Travis walked up with an armful of his own.

"It always baffled me," Travis said, tossing the buckets in the wagon. "Every home in town has one of these buckets. We even painted them red specifically so they would be kept apart and not lost in the barn or tucked back in some honey house somewhere. And yet, every time we finish up, the fire is out, the people are gone, but the buckets remain."

Chancy smiled. "Easier to sort through 'em down at the church than hunt through the dark, I reckon."

"I suppose," Travis said. "Though you watch. Next time there's a day fire, it'll be just the same."

Chancy paused and looked at him. "Sounds like you're thinking the same thoughts I am."

Travis raised an eyebrow. "I may not share all my thoughts with the people, but you and I seem to frequently agree. 'Next time' likely won't be too far away, do you think?"

"Fire every other day?" Chancy considered it. "I suppose it ain't unheard of. Get a dry spell, old wood. Sorta begging for something to catch. But, yeah, these seem to be a little more consistent than what I'd expect."

"The layout as well," Travis said. "Where we are now, this is where I would expect the fires. This side of town is the oldest. Granted, you can ride across Elkhorn and not see much variation in the ages of the buildings, a decade maybe. But these here are the very first buildings to have gone up. The haberdashery, or what's left of it, started out as the mercantile and post office before those moved closer to the center of town.

If it were just the oldest, driest wood, all the buildings around here should've gone up. A lot of them have. This wasn't originally a stand-alone building, in fact. Used to be just one third of the original structure."

"And yet," Chancy said, "we've had that fire on the north side, the south, and now the east. You betting on west next?"

Travis paused for a moment. "It would seem things lean that way. As for now, though, other than telling folks to keep their buckets at the ready, I'm not sure what else to tell them."

"Tell 'em to take their buckets home with 'em." Chancy grinned.

"I choose my battles, Chancy," Travis laughed.

"Probably wise. If I had to guess, a battle's what we're gonna be coming up against sooner rather than later."

"The thought has crossed my mind," Travis said. "I knew we'd have trouble once Frank was gone, but typically it's like what we were dealing with before. Unorganized. Weak. Flashes in the pan that eventually wear themselves out. With the townsfolk keeping an eye on things, I was hoping the problems would've died down by now."

"Well, they ain't quite what they was, but I'm not sure this is the change I's hoping to see."

"Any word on the Renfrew boy?" Travis asked, leaning on the edge of the wagon.

"Nah," Chancy wiped his hands on his trousers. "He's gone, but that's about all anybody can say about it. Rumor was he'd been talkin' about doin' something big, but don't nobody knows precisely what. Pal of his said Carl had his eye on some girl he was looking to impress, so I can't imagine he just up and left. Especially not with that farm he got when his daddy passed. But when a man up and disappears out here, there ain't much we can do but keep our eyes and ears open."

"Been out to talk with Ship?"

Chancy sighed, a tired smile on his face. "A couple times, actually. But I bet you can guess what he had to say."

"They don't know anything?"

"Practically word for word," Chancy said. "You'd have a better chance of prying a fish out of a snapper's mouth than getting anything useful from that place. Every one of 'em must be blind and deaf."

"Yes," Travis mused. "But all we can do is keep kicking over rocks for the moment. Something's bound to turn up."

"After this long, it's more'n likely to be a body."

"I'm afraid you're probably right. I've been trying to figure out how to get rid of that place since I took this office," Travis said. "But it's a mystery. Folks don't like it there, but not enough to do anything about it. So long as Ship's got his men taken care of, the whole place seems to function like it's in another town."

"The local thieves' den," Chancy said.

Travis nodded. "Unfortunately, yes."

"You don't suppose they're involved with these fires, do ya?"

"Doubtful. Like I said, they seem to have some kind of regulations all their own. The trouble they do cause is usually elsewhere, and even when it's here, there's no way to tie it to them. If they were involved, it would be a huge change of pace for them. You saw for yourself what happened with them when McFarland was around."

"A whole lotta nothing, as far as I could tell," Chancy said.

"Myself as well," Travis replied. "I don't know if McFarland had a deal with them, or if he tried to set one up and decided it wasn't worth it, but Ship deals only with himself and his people."

"So, we got a whole new problem on our hands."

"That's my guess. Someone is making moves. The problem is, for now, it's impossible to say who. And as you said, three fires in six days… it's uncommon, but it's not unheard of."

Chancy smiled at the man. "We both know this ain't just poor luck."

"Yes," Travis sighed. "For the moment, all we can do is try to keep up."

"Well," Chancy said, taking off his hat and wiping his brow, "that don't sound like much of a plan to me."

"It isn't," Travis said. "I'm calling another meeting at the church tomorrow. The people seemed happy enough to help last time we asked, and this will be at least slightly more straightforward."

"Organizing yourself a fire brigade?"

"I don't know if I'd call it organizing," Travis said. "They seem to do rather well on their own. Perhaps just endorsing. The townsfolk are showing some commitment here. They want what we want. This might be more of just a pat on the back and encouragement to keep doing what they're doing."

"Ah," Chancy said. "Congratulate 'em, keep 'em happy."

Travis shrugged. "When people are proud of their town, they fight for it. You've seen that firsthand yourself on more than one occasion. What we need to do, if you'll pardon the expression, is keep their fires burning. Keep them motivated. Let them know their efforts are noticed, appreciated, and not for nothing."

Chancy nodded. "Ain't hurt nothing, I reckon. Catch more flies with honey than vinegar, as they say."

Travis laughed. "It's not the catching I'm worried about, at least not with this aspect. It's keeping them around. Every town has its ups and downs. We need to make sure Elkhorn stays on the positive side of that. Too many downs and a town loses its people."

"I ain't given up yet," Chancy said, walking off to gather up more fire buckets.

***

Back in the sheriff's station, Chancy found Jack Wallace posted up on the front porch, feet on the rails.

"Get 'er put out?" Jack called as Chancy walked up.

"Yeah," Chancy sighed. "That one anyhow."
"You're expecting more too, huh?"

"You, me, the mayor. I don't like to jump at things, but I feel like something's brewing here."

"I know what ya mean," Jack said. "Fires spread out like this. It seems too organized."

"My thoughts exactly," Chancy said.

"Well…" Jack took his feet down and stood up. "How about some good news?" He beckoned the sheriff into the station. "Things ain't precisely as they were, but we're darn close."

Chancy walked around the office, paying particular attention to the flooring where the worst of the first fire had been. "Ain't too shabby," he said, walking over to look at the window repairs. "Maybe we shoulda done this ourselves sooner." He grinned.

"Free, too," Jack said. "I don't know what you done, but you certainly got a way of bringing out the good in folks."

Chancy laughed. "I don't know about that. If I was a bettin' man, I'd wager these people just want to make sure there's a place to stick their outlaws when we bring 'em in. A sheriff ain't much good without a jail."

"Maybe," Jack said, "But the jail was all right. Most of the damage was up here in the office. And we don't spend a whole lotta time just sitting around here these days."

"About that," Chancy walked over and sat behind the desk, his old familiar chair still waiting for him. "Any word on Carl Renfrew?"

Jack shook his head. "No more than we've ever had. Went by the Shipyard, but I think it's safe to say we about wore out our welcome there. What little of one we had to begin with."

"Yeah," Chancy said. "Mayor don't think Ship's boys got anything to do with the fires. You been around quite a spell though. What d'you think?"

Jack put a boot up on the extra chair, leaning his elbows on his knees. "Tell you the truth, I was kinda hoping it was them boys. Finally give us a reason to run 'em out. Shoot, if we were really lucky, they'd screw around and burn their own place down. But I'm gonna side with the mayor on this one. I don't seem 'em getting involved with things this close to home."

"You got any guess on who would, then?"

Jack sighed and shook his head. "Out here, could be anybody. We're open for business now that Frank's gone, but the way the folks've been stepping up, I'm really hoping word'll get out, and this'll be the last attempt for a while."

"We been hoping that for a while, too. Seems to be the only thing that lasts," Chancy said. "I reckon we just keep pluggin' along till someone's fool enough to say something they oughtn't."

"I was thinkin'," Jack said. "Something like this. If it were our own folks, we'd know about it already. We got half the town coming by here or the mayor's office, turnin' in news about things we don't even have laws for. If it was somebody we knew, well, we'da heard. My money's on a new face in town."

"Plenty of those to choose from."

"Yeah, but I'm thinking, what if it ain't a new face entirely?"

"What d'ya mean?"

"Well…" Jack grinned. "I don't mean to be insinuatin' nothing, but I'd venture to say you've made an enemy or two in your day."

Chancy laughed. "Yeah, a couple, I reckon."

"Anybody spring to mind?"

"You think this is about me and not the town?"

"I don't know what to think for sure," Jack said. "I'm just thinking. It ain't far-fetched."

Chancy sat for a moment, chewing on the idea. Could he have really brought more trouble just by trying to help out? He supposed it made sense in some ways. "It's a thought, I s'pose."

"But?"

"But most of the men I tracked down are dead or locked up."

Jack nodded. "Yeah, I kinda figured that." He stood up, hitching his thumbs in his belt. "Just keep your eyes open. I'd hate to have us put in all these hours and find out we were looking in the wrong direction the whole time."

"I ain't the only one with enemies," Chancy said, looking at the man.

"You're right there," Jack said. "But mine aren't so far-flung as yours. As for now, I need to get me some grub and find a place to bed down for a few hours. You got everything under control here?"

"Yeah," Chancy sighed. "I'll come find ya if I need ya."

"You do that," Jack said. "And like I told ya, look for familiar faces. Plenty of people'd love to take down the great Chancy Rosman."

Chancy laughed. "Get outta here before I decide to make you stay."

With a wave, Jack stepped out into the morning air, and Chancy pulled a stack of papers across the desk. The deputy had a point, he thought. But to try to remember everyone who could want to put a bullet in him, every person who had some kind of beef... Well, that would make for a very long list.

Chapter 6
The Signal

As the tiring days wore on, only one more fire popped up at an old abandoned barn on the west side of town. It completed the pattern, covering the fourth direction of the compass, but it seemed a half-hearted attempt.

After the meeting with the mayor, the citizens had become more motivated and organized, staying on top of outbreaks to the extent that only the outer range of town had been available for this type of arson.

Chancy was pleased with their work, but wondered how long it would last. They were still only dealing with problems as they arose and not getting any closer to the source of the trouble, or finding out who was behind the arson.

He didn't like to hope, but a small part of him wondered if things might eventually wear themselves out. Part of the mayor's meeting, something that hadn't been intended by either Travis or Chancy but had come up at the suggestions of Mr. Nichols, involved a kind of rotating nightly patrol.

Chancy wasn't overly keen on the idea of the citizens acting with any kind of jurisdiction, but as Travis had said when explaining it the next day, the folks were already out. They were already bringing in good information. The choice was to either support the patrols and benefit or try to put a stop to something that wouldn't be stopped.

The logic was there, but the sheriff didn't feel completely comfortable with it. They already had the unchecked rogues to deal with. Adding a battalion of unchecked and interested townsfolk to the mix didn't just seem unwise, it seemed dangerous.

"That's why we have a signal," Travis had said. "Three shots in the air. If we're lucky, it'll be enough to startle anybody involved and send them on their way. If not, folks know to hang back till you or one of the deputies arrive."

"You know there's a third option," Chancy had said.

"What's that?"

"These fellas hear the three shots and decide to stay and fight. I'm all for folks being wary and keeping their eyes open, but we don't wanna start getting too big for our britches here. These are just regular people. They ain't gonna be worth much in a shootout."

Travis raised an eyebrow.

"Okay," Chancy said. "I get it. They came through for Teresa that day. But that was different. We were organized. They had a plan to follow. This here…" He shook his head. "I just don't know."

"Well," Travis told him, "for the time being, just try it out. Who knows? You may be right, and the first time shots are fired we realize this is a terrible idea. But we've got them on the run, Chancy. I can feel it. Now it's time for that final push."

***

Chancy leaned back in his chair, his boots up on the corner of the desk. The conversation with Travis had turned out to be a moot point. Sure, the warning system had worked a handful of times, but it still left them pushing against minor incidents.

They didn't have a common enemy to push out. And more than once, Chancy had found himself the unexpected recipient of an outlaw shoved through his office door by two or three of the patrolmen in the middle of the night.

Part of the deal had been there would be at least four, but no more than six men in each of the watch parties. The number seemed intimidating enough to keep most of the violence at bay, but not so outlandish as to bring on an all-out melee.

What Chancy was seeing more often than not was the party of six splintering into groups of two or three. And in fairness, he would've done the same in a different situation. It made it easier to move around, simpler to cover more ground.

But he'd been a bounty hunter for more years than he cared to remember. These men were tailors, apothecaries, and stableboys.

And there was another problem with the plan, one he'd only discussed with Jack Wallace so far, but the two men had agreed and were waiting in anticipation since they'd first discussed it. When the three shots rang out in the dark, quiet night, Chancy wondered if the problem had finally come into play.

The sheriff bolted from his chair at the sound. It came from the west, though it didn't sound as far off as the barn fire had been. A few of the men in the cells down the hall cheered, having already realized what the signal meant. Something was going on, and whether they got to be a part of it or not, whether it even was a successful crime, they loved to see the lawmen being run ragged.

"Go get 'em, boss!" Chancy heard one man jeer, followed by the cackles of a few others.

He stepped out onto the porch, almost immediately confronted by a group of three patrollers.

"What's the plan, Chancy?" one of them asked, breathless but clearly excited.

No matter how many times he'd told them to stay put, the men had taken to following closer at his heels. Chancy paused for a moment and looked at them. "You oughtta know what's going on more'n I do," he said. "Aren't your orders to stay as a group and only fire shots to alert me? Less you all ran fast as that echo, seems like you're already messing up the plan."

"Aw, Sheriff, you know we do better split up like this," a man said. "'Sides, now you got us three to watch your back."

Chancy hesitated for a moment. He'd sent Jack home hours earlier, hoping the man could get some rest during the night hours for once, but undoubtedly the deputy had heard the shots and was likely preparing to be or already was on his way toward the noise.

If Jack had left from his house up on the north side, they'd converge to the west from two angles. Trying to meet him halfway would be pointless and possibly leave Jack racing into danger on his own. Chancy wasn't concerned. The man couldn't fend for himself, but it seemed against all sense to try to muddy the waters by not heading straight to the source of the problem.

"Look," he glanced over at the men as he walked to his horse. "You all need to hang back. I know you ain't gonna listen if I tell you to stay, but you best keep out of sight till I figure out what's going on. Ain't no sense in one of you catching a bullet. Especially since it'd most likely come from your other trigger-happy patrollers."

There was a brief sound of laughter before the men realized how true the sheriff's words might be.

"We'll hang back," he heard one of them, it sounded like Mr. Johnson, say. "But you need us, we'll be close."

"Not too close," Chancy said, throwing his leg up over the saddle.

"You got it."

Chancy gave the men one last glance, shook his head slightly, and rode off toward the shots.

The sound of the horses' hooves were clear and rhythmic on the dark streets. It was well past midnight, and the shops had been closed for hours. Even the saloons were typically winding up business by this time, but up ahead, Chancy could make out flickering lights on the side of one of the taller buildings.

They weren't flames, or at least not the flames of a building fire. These were smaller and moving more erratically. Torches, he thought. Though whether they were for light or for starting a fire, he couldn't be sure.

He slowed the Appaloosa to a trot and then a walk as he got closer, his eyes sweeping back and forth across the street for the other three patrollers. If they had any sense, they'd be hunkered down in the shadows at the very least. Of course, if they had any sense, he would have passed them already on their way to find him. He reined in the horse a few storefronts down from the flickering shadows and climbed out of the saddle.

Voices drifted back to him, but they were garbled, sounding half-drunk. He unholstered his revolver, holding the barrel up but not cocking the hammer yet. Something felt off about the situation.

He strained his ears to pick out any clear words in the sounds coming toward him and kept his eyes moving along the shadows and door frames on either side of him. He crept forward to within about twenty feet of the alley, hunkering down behind a rain barrel to try to assess his surroundings.

From the darkness, a voice whispered out to him. "Something ain't right."

Chancy grinned to himself. "How'd you beat me here, Jack?"

"Sleep in my clothes most nights lately," the deputy said, moving over from the alleyway to crouch down next to the sheriff.

"What you seen so far?" Chancy asked.

"Same as you," the man said. "Carousing, it sounds like. I didn't wanna move till I figured out where the fellas were who fired the shots, but I ain't seen anybody but you so far."

"Yeah, well..." Chancy gestured with his head in the direction behind them.

"Split patrols?"

"Yeah," Chancy said. "Three of 'em were outside the office when I came out. I figured the other three'd be up here. You ain't heard anything? Nobody hollerin' for help? Nothing?"

"Just this," Jack said.

Chancy stayed still for a moment, then slowly stood up. "We ain't gonna learn anything behind a rain barrel, I reckon. You cross over to the far side there. Stay up with me, but hang back outta sight as much as ya can till we figure out what's going on."

Jack nodded and slipped across the street, almost immediately blending into the shadows cast by the overhang of the storefronts.

Chancy walked out toward the middle of the street, keeping his gun pointed up but hoping to make himself visible in the moonlight. If the men were going to shoot at him, he supposed they would've by now.

With any luck, this was just a case of late-night revelry gone out of hand. There was intermittent laughter among the voices, and the general tone seemed offhand enough. The men certainly weren't trying to hide anything, at least.

Still, it seemed strange. Why gather round in the alley in the middle of the night? Why not head off to a ranch, a bunkhouse? And more importantly, why the shots? Travis had been explicit in his instructions. Two quick shots followed by a pause, then a third. The odd timing was intended to distinguish the signal from any kind of more violent gunplay, which was sporadic and typically involved more than just the three reports. But Chancy had heard it just as clearly as Jack had, as had the other patrolmen. Three shots spaced correctly, then no more.

He plodded ahead, assuming Jack was staying with him and hoping the three others were keeping a safe distance. Finally, he stepped to the end of the alleyway, into the light of what appeared to be a small campfire in the middle of the dusty path.

Three men stood around it, one with a torch raised, helping illuminate the other two, one hunkered down by the fire, and the other standing off to the side, a jug hanging from his finger.

"What's going on here, fellas?" Chancy said in a casual tone, hoping to not startle any of them into action.

The man by the fire looked over and laughed. "Well, howdy, Sheriff. What brings you to this neck of the woods?"

Chancy paused at the words, then looked the men over as best he could from the distance in the flickering light. All three had guns strapped to their hips, though none had made even the slightest move toward the weapons. "Y'all need to clear out of here," Chancy said slowly. "Can't be having fires like this. You know as well as I do, places 'round here been acting more and more likely to catch."

The man with the jug snickered. "Funny thing, ain't it?"

Chancy kept his eyes moving over the men. "What're you fellas up to, anyway?"

"Ah, just havin' a palaver," the man with the torch said. "Sharing some stories. Sharing some whiskey. Damn town's closed up too early for us, so we figured we'd make our own selves a spot here."

It was nonsense, obviously, and besides the man with the jug, the other two seemed completely sober. Or at least sober for this hour of the night.

"Who fired the shots?" Chancy asked.

"Shots?" the man by the fire asked, grinning. "What shots? We didn't fire no shots."

Chancy approached the three slowly, keeping his eyes moving between their hands. "There were three shots," he said. "Not fifteen minutes ago. Came from this direction. Now I ain't seen nobody on my way over, so if y'all could be so kind as to let me check out your firearms, I'd be much obliged."

It was a long gamble, and he knew it. Odds were whoever had fired the shots would've reloaded immediately, both to cover his tracks and to cover his hide. It didn't do to wander about with a half-loaded gun.

Chancy moved closer to the man crouching by the fire. "May as well start with you, fella," he said.

"With me?" the man laughed. "What'd I do to bring down the law on me? I's just sitting." Then, so fast the motion was blurred in the flickering light, Chancy saw the man reach down and draw.

The sheriff brought his gun down to fire on the man when he caught the quick, continued motion.

The man spun the revolver on his finger once, twice, then twisted it about, ending with the barrel in his hand, the butt pointed out toward Chancy.

"That's a good way to get yourself shot," the sheriff said.

The man laughed. "I'm just playing about. No harm, Sheriff." He grinned. "Fast though, warn't it? I think I'da had you if I wanted."

"Not quite," Jack said, emerging from the shadows, his gun still pointed at the man by the fire.

"Ahh," the fellow laughed. "That's clever. That's clever right there. First y'all got your rats. Now you got your patrols. Now you're sneaking about in the shadows. Hell, it's gonna be tough to tell the good uns from the bad uns if you get much more clever." He gestured with his gun toward Chancy. "Well, go on. Ain't ya gonna take it? Check and see if I been firing off anything?"

Chancy hesitated, looking at Jack, who shrugged. "Y'all get on outta here," Chancy said, brushing the man's proffered gun away. "Next time I come 'cross you, you'll be coming back with me."

The three men lingered for a moment, then began kicking dirt over the small campfire.

"Seems to me you got things all wrong," the fellow with the jug said between pulls at the neck.

"How's that?" Chancy asked.

"Well," the man smiled. "You spendin' your time here hasslin' us when you still ain't got a clue who was shooting off for help a bit ago. Where's your patrols at?"

Chancy stepped across the struggling flames and grabbed the man by the collar of his shirt, pushing him back up against the wall of one building. "That's a darn good question," he said between clenched teeth. "And it seems to me like maybe you got some answers."

The man smiled, looking over Chancy's shoulder at the other two men. Just then, shots rang out again. Two quick, a pause, then a third. Chancy looked over at Jack.

"From the north," Jack said, already working his way back down the alley toward the main street.

Chancy hesitated for a moment, the man still pinned against the wall under his tight grip.

"You better hurry, Sheriff," the man said, holding in his laugher. "Sounds like somebody needs ya."

Chancy fought the urge to smack the smirk off the man's face. "I best not be seeing you again," he said, pushing the man to the side and walking back out toward the street where Jack was. "Any of you," he called over his shoulder.

"Oh, sure, boss," he heard one of them say, the words echoing like those from the cell earlier.

He caught up with Jack one storefront down, where the deputy was unhitching his horse from a dark side street.

"What do you think?" Jack said as the man walked up.

"Same as you, I reckon," Chancy said.

"They've got us over a barrel."

"Damn!" Chancy punched his fist into the palm of his other hand. "I knew this was gonna happen. I told you it was."

"Aye," Jack said. "And I agree with ya. But there ain't much we can do about it in this moment." He looked over Chancy's shoulders, where a few shadows were moving in the street. "Might wanna send them fellas home though, 'fore they get theirselves shot."

Chancy looked back to see the trio of patrolmen slowly approaching him and Jack.

"What's the plan?" one man asked. "We split up? You want us to stay and tail these fellas?"

Chancy took off his hat, doing his best to control his anger at the situation.

"I want y'all to get," he said. "Ain't no place for you out here, especially the way this night's shaping up. Get yourselves home and stay there. I catch any of you out, I'm bringing you in with me."

"What?" the man protested. "We're here to help you. We were told by the mayor.

"The mayor told you to stick with your patrol. The mayor told you to fire your signal shots and stay outta the way. Looks to me like you either abandoned your pals or you're giving me the run around. Either way, I ain't got no use for ya."

"You take that back," the man said.

"I ain't got time for this," Chancy said. "Get off the streets or you end up in the cells. Go on." He waved his hand at the men. "Take it up with Travis if you got a problem."

He turned back to Jack as the men, grumbling, slowly made their way back up the street.

"What is the plan, Chance?"

The sheriff sighed. "Only got one option. Follow the shots. We stick together, though. I ain't making this any worse than it already is."

***

The next morning, Chancy and Jack sat in the sheriff's station, tired, irritable, and in no mood for the discussion the mayor was trying to have with them.

"I understand," Travis was saying, "that you don't want the patrolmen interfering. And I understand that they had broken up when they were supposed to stay together. But I just don't know if abolishing the patrol altogether is the best idea."

"Look," Chancy said, running his hands over his tired face. "I ain't saying it's the best, but I ain't saying it's the worst either. You gotta look at the situation for what it is, though. You're a smart fella. I'll be the first to say so. But you ain't the only smart fella, and that's where we're gonna run into trouble. Where we did run into trouble."

"You said yourself it all led to nothing, though," Travis said.

"That's exactly the point," Jack spoke up from his chair by the desk. "They got our number now. Literally. The number is three. We covered more miles in this town last night than I care to think about. Time we got to where one set of shots went off, we had about five minutes to catch our breath before three more wrung out on the other side of town. They're just runnin' us, Mayor, for the fun of it. And the way things are right now, we ain't got no choice but to follow them shots. You get rid of your boys, though, even for a night, and things might change."

Travis sighed. "Pulling back now could only be a sign of weakness. They'll see they've got us figured out."

"They already see that," Chancy said. "What we gotta do is keep 'em from thinking we're stupid, too. Long as we got patrols out there, we don't know who's firing signals. We don't know which ones are real, which ones are distractions. For all we know, by tonight, half the town's gonna be firing three shots just to try it out.

"Now, I've supported you throughout all these changes, but you knowed from the get-go it was only till things stopped bein' beneficial. All's that's happenin' now is we're gettin' run more ragged than we was before. We couldn't keep up with all the complaints comin' in. On top of that, there was the fires. Now these fake signals. Whether or not you like it, we ain't made anything better with what we been trying, so it's time to try something else."

"And what might that be?" the mayor asked, standing up and walking over to the window. "These towns can be powder kegs, Chancy. You know that as well as I do. And the thing is, we never know what's going to set it off. We've got the people on our side, in a force like I've not seen before. Telling them to sit back might not be something they want to hear. Especially with things still seeming so out of control."

"Things are out of control because of the people," Jack snorted. "Too many chiefs, Mayor. You know the saying as well as anybody."

"It seems we either have too many or not enough," the mayor said, looking out at the street. "Which would you prefer?"

Chancy held up a hand before Jack could reply.

"Look," the sheriff said. "How about this? Let's do a trial run. One night. How long you need to track down all your patrolmen?"

The mayor turned back to the sheriff, walking across the room and sitting back down in a chair next to Jack. "I suppose we could do it by this evening."

"Good. Track 'em down and tell 'em we got a plan. Don't spook 'em. Don't make 'em think we don't want 'em anymore."

"Which you don't," the mayor said.

"Which I don't know about yet," Chancy said. "All I know is I can't keep track of every man, woman, and child in this town. Go find your men and tell them to hunker down tonight. If I know any of them are out, me and the deputies can't do our job. And if any of them are out, I'm gonna assume they're trying to prevent us from doing so."

"Well, what is the plan?" Travis asked. "Can I at least know that?"

"To be quite honest with you, sir, for the moment, I'd like to keep that between me, Jack, Clay and Burl here," Chancy said. "Less folks know, the less they can tell."

"Are you saying you don't trust me?"

Chancy smiled. "It ain't that at all, sir, and I think you know it."

The mayor sighed again. "Fine," he said, finally. "Do what you need to do. I'll make sure everyone stays inside tonight. Any of them you catch out, bring them back here, and I'll deal with them personally in the morning. We need to get this taken care of, Chancy. Fast."

Rosman nodded, stood and shook the mayor's hand, then watched as the man walked out into the morning.

Jack removed his hat and tossed it over onto the seat so recently occupied by Mayor Travis. "You didn't make him any too happy there, Chance. Sure that's wise?"

"Wise or not, I ain't got a lot of choice in the matter. But this way, ain't gonna be nobody saying I'm ordering folks around. Word comes from Travis. Hopefully they'll listen."

"So what's the big plan, then?" Clay grinned. "Or are you still working on it?"

Chancy allowed himself a small laugh. "Oh, I got it figured out. Don't know if you'd really call it a plan, per se. Maybe the lack of one, though."

Burl leaned forward. "I wondered as much. No wonder you didn't wanna tell Travis."

Chancy shrugged. "If you got a better idea, I'm open to suggestions. But the way I see it, the only way to deal with the signal problem is to show 'em we don't care about the signals anymore. So long as we know our boys ain't the ones shooting off out there, I don't see any reason we need to go look into it."

"And once they see we aren't interested anymore, they'll give up on it."

"Well, ya see, that's the beauty of it. Whether or not they give up on it don't really matter much to me. So long as I hear that signal from here on out, all I know is some fella's got three less bullets than he did before. I hope they all start trying it out."

"What're you gonna tell Travis, though?"

"I reckon I got all night to think of something."

"Gonna be a loud night."

"Maybe," Chancy said. "How long would you keep it up, though? I figure they'll try twice, three times. Once they see we ain't gonna come running anymore, ain't much sense in keeping up the charade."

"One way to deal with it," Jack said.

"Like I told ya," Chancy said. "I'm open to suggestions. This just seemed like the way that kept us from chasing ghosts all evening."

"What about after that, though?" Burl asked. "We might buy ourselves a night, saving us some nonsense in the future, but it still ain't solving any problems."

"I know it," Chancy said. "That's what's been driving me up the walls. We got folks coming in left and right with tips and gossip, but it ain't none of it solving our bigger problem."

"The fires," Jack said, the words more a statement than a question.

"The fires," Chancy said. "What happened to the Renfrew boy. What's brewing just beneath the surface. I hate to say it, but I wonder sometimes if the mayor oughtta be putting as much trust in these folks as he does."

Jack gave him a sidelong look. "I don't know if I'd take it that far yet. Sure, they ain't the best-trained men, but they got their hearts in the right place."

"What about that signal, though? You don't think somebody let the news of that slip out?"

Jack smiled slightly. "C'mon, Chancy. I don't mean to speak ill, but you know as well as I do that wasn't exactly the most complicated thing to figure out. Once is chance, twice is coincidence, three times a pattern. That signal never had a chance of workin' after the first night."

"You seemed to go along with it," Chancy said.

"I go along with the mayor," the man said. "And I go along with you. If the signal had worked, I'd be surprised as anybody, but I'd also be glad it did." He shrugged. "Sometimes you just gotta keep throwing things till you see what sticks."

Chancy sat quietly for a moment, chewing on the deputy's words. "I just ain't much for sitting around and waiting," he said finally.

"No," Jack agreed. "I ain't either. But we also can't go out there half-cocked and expecting it to have any good come of it."

"I don't suppose so."

"I'll tell you one thing that maybe you forgot," Jack said, looking over at Chancy. "Somebody always screws up. You seen it when you were a bounty hunter. I seen it here in town. Shoot, we seen it just now with our own mayor. That plan of his, sure, it seemed like a good idea at the moment, but you think he'd call it anything but a screwup now? And he's the one running the show here. Or supposed to be, leastwise.

"Now you're gonna sit there and tell me you think whoever's out there gunnin' for Frank's old spot ain't gonna screw up, too? I ain't never met a man smart enough to never make a mistake."

Chancy smiled. The man's vigor was encouraging. And his point was valid. Eventually, everyone made a mistake. He just hoped it was sooner.

The mayor had already shown himself as overeager, ready to jump at any opportunity. A man like that could be exploited and, in some ways, already had, after the fiasco with the signal shots.

"I suppose they did already make one mistake," Chancy said.

"What's that?" Clay asked.

"They seem to think we aren't gonna be sitting here ready for 'em."

Jack grinned. "A fatal mistake indeed."

Chapter 7
All in a Week

While Chancy's prediction regarding the signal proved to be accurate, his plan of action, or perhaps inaction, had one unexpected outcome. The sheer oddness of his choice, the disappearance of both the lawmen and the citizen patrol, seemed to spook the outlaws.

They committed not a single crime in the course of the patrol-less night. If Chancy had to guess, he would have said the men were all waiting for a trap to be sprung, and he was more than happy to have a quiet night in the office.

Unfortunately, those twelve quiet hours were much too fleeting. Like a kid poking at a stray dog, the lawbreakers started inching closer into town again the next afternoon and over the course of the following week.

The confusion Chancy had given them was forgotten and replaced with a growing brazenness. Once the signal had been abandoned, things quickly came full circle and, despite how useless the three shots had been, Chancy wished they had worked.

Folks had to hope to find Chancy in town. He had to do his best to head where he thought he was most needed. The larger, actual fires had stayed at bay for the time being, but it was the smaller issues that were eating up his days.

Often, while dealing with one problem, another citizen would come up with a complaint or news or some bit of information that may or may not be a lead, and Chancy would find himself stuck in one section of town for most of the day.

That would've been fine if he'd had enough men to divide the town up, give each area its own full-time deputy, but between only Chancy and his three deputies, there were always large sections of town left to its own devices.

Thankfully, the patrol Travis had set up had been content to sit on their hands. Whether this was because of a misunderstanding and the men thought hanging back was the new, indefinite order, Chancy couldn't be sure.

The fact of the matter was, though, even if he grudgingly missed the idea of the signal, he in no way longed to return to the days of skittish townsfolk roaming the streets with loaded guns at all hours.

Chancy had invested himself in the town. He'd given his time and his blood, and he wasn't about to let the citizens shoot themselves in the foot by acting too brashly. If that meant he had to handle this on his own, so be it.

Besides—he thought back to Frank's end—there were always a few men he knew he could count on. Unfortunately, they seemed to be the men who had avoided patrol duty when possible, seeming to know they were not offering a service so much as a nuisance to the man.

Over the next few days, Chancy worked more and more on his own, keeping Jack, Clay and Burl abreast of details when he needed to for both safety and to use the deputies as sounding boards.

Beyond Jack though, only Teresa was allowed into the man's mind. Even Mayor Travis, Deputy Blount and Deputy Newcom were kept at arm's length. Chancy didn't care for it, but he knew he needed to keep his future options open.

If things didn't straighten up soon, he could foresee himself stepping a little further outside the law than the mayor could ignore.

***

Across town, in Anne-Marie's office, Harm Swally found himself yet again occupying the armchair across the desk. The difference was, the more times he found himself in the room, the more comfortable he became.

This new arrangement, starting with the fires, had put them on a more equal standing. He still didn't trust the woman, but he was seeing that she could get things done. And line his pockets in the process.

He'd lit plenty of fires in his past, but none had paid like the fires for Anne-Marie. The woman must've had bottomless coffers. Harm knew the stories that were working their way around town: that Anne-Marie had been the one to double-cross Frank McFarland, that she was in cahoots with Mayor Travis , that this whole thing was a scheme to… well, no one ever seemed to know what benefit a mayor could have by lighting his own town on fire, but Harm was sure if he thought long enough, he could come up with one.

None of that mattered to him, anyway. What mattered now was the bills in his pockets, the men in the town, and the bottle of whiskey on the desk. He'd been doing a fine job, he knew, and he felt this might be the perfect time to ensure Anne-Marie knew as well.

He poured himself a few fingers of liquor, topping off her glass as well. The gentlemanly move seemed to have little impact on the woman, perhaps because he was attempting to be so chivalrous with her own bottle.

He pulled a tobacco pouch from inside his leather vest, rolling a lumpy cigarette as he settled back in the chair. The woman looked on with amused, if not entirely interested, eyes.

Harm had called this meeting himself, and she was curious to see just what the little man had to say. "Comfortable?" she asked finally as Harm attempted to blow smoke rings up toward the ceiling.

"In some ways, yes," he said, bringing his gaze down to her. "In others, not so much."

Anne-Marie reached out and brought her glass of whiskey closer, taking a demure sip, waiting. If the man wanted to talk, he could talk, but she certainly would not pander to him.

"Ya see, here's the thing." Harm leaned forward in his seat slightly. "I done lit your fires. I been raisin' your kinda hell. Every decent man in this town is running around like a chicken with its head cut off. And I'll be honest with ya, I've enjoyed every minute." He laughed, taking a swallow of his drink.

"I'm glad you enjoy your work," Anne-Marie said. "It's important."

Harm paused, unsure if she meant his enjoyment or the work itself was important. He supposed she probably meant the latter, but for the moment, he wanted to feel appreciated.

"I got some questions though," he said finally. "You promised me Chancy Rosman at the beginning of this deal, and I been patient about it. I had that son of a gun in my sights more than once in the last couple weeks, and I never pulled the trigger. And you know why?"

"Because I'd have you shot?"

Harm settled back in his seat, trying to suppress a startled look. "Well, that's one way to look at it, I reckon," he said. "I was gonna say it's outta respect to you. Not everybody'd cotton to a gal ordering him around, but I tell you, I ain't got time for that sense. Somebody's smart, somebody's takin' care of me, I take care of them. Simple as that."

Anne-Marie took another sip of her drink in order to cover the smile arising at the man's obvious nonsense and pandering. "So what is your complaint, Mr. Swally? My timeline?"

"Well, to be honest with you, yeah. Or at least," he backtracked, "it's more so just that I don't rightly know what your timeline is. Now I took you at your word. I was gonna get Rosman. And I s'pose it's my fault for not getting more details before I signed on, but..." He trailed off, unsure whether he should demand or be curious. Finally, as Harm usually did, he avoided all tact and chose the blunt option. "When are you gonna let me do that?"

"Shoot him?'

"Shoot him. Stab him. Blow him up. Throw him off a cliff. Don't rightly matter much to me how I do it, long as he knows it's me doing it."

"You'd like a day? Perhaps a time?"

Harm couldn't be sure, but it felt like the woman was mocking him. The fact was, though, those were exactly the things he wanted. "Well, yeah," he said after a moment. "I don't mind doing your dirty work. I don't even mind not knowing exactly why you're doing what you're doing. But a feller don't like working too long when he don't even know about his payday."

Anne-Marie sat her glass back on the desk, adjusted her dress on her knee, and looked across at the man, purposefully drawing out the silence. "I suppose," she said at last, "that is not an entirely unreasonable request, and truth be told, you've done a fine job, Mr. Swally."

The man smiled awkwardly.

"But there are some things you should know. First, this is my office, in what will shortly be my town. That is my chair you're sitting in and my whiskey in your glass. My money lines your pockets. You are a tool. I am keeping you around because you are reliable. If you prove otherwise, you'll be replaced. It has nothing to do with who you are. In fact, in most ways, I really couldn't care less, but we have an agreement that benefits us both, and that is of value to me.

"However," her tone became darker, "agreements come and go. So I would encourage you to remember which side of the desk you're sitting on. One of us can make demands, Mr. Swally, and it is not you. Should I decide to keep you on indefinitely, that's what I'll do. Should you decide to make a move of your own, don't forget who knows every single match you've sparked around here lately. It wouldn't take but a moment for some of that information to slip out, and with the folks here lining up to rat on one another, I'm sure you'd find yourself right close to your pal Rosman before you knew what hit you."

"That a threat?" Harm said, though his small voice did little to exude confidence.

"Yes, it is," Anne-Marie said. "It is a threat. It is a promise. A simple fact is what it is. I find it beneficial to not dance about an issue. These are the truths of our agreement. If you don't like them, that is unfortunate. Nevertheless, it's too late now." The woman leaned back in her chair, pausing for a moment to ensure he was listening closely and not simply waiting to rattle off some other useless claptrap. "That being said," she began again, "you have been doing a fine job, and I suppose it is fair that a man be allowed some kind of goal. If you're willing to work with me."

"Don't see as I have much of a choice," Harm muttered.

"That's the spirit," Anne-Marie laughed. "But I promise you, Harm, things will be splendid in the end. How does one week sound?"

"One week of what?"

"One more week of whatever I need," she said. "Then you're free to pursue the sheriff, however you see fit."

"Week's a long time," he mused. "Lot could happen in that amount of time."

Anne-Marie laughed again. "A month ago, you weren't even looking for this man. Don't play games with me, Harm.

Besides, if you can keep yourself alive that long, surely you can protect your prize."

Harm shook his head. Surely he didn't hear her right. He was supposed to tear the town apart, but protect the sheriff at the same time? Just so he could kill him later? It didn't add up.

Anne-Marie let the man stew for a moment. Not only did she have to admit she enjoyed watching the gears attempt to turn in the man's head, but there was a part of her that simply liked the sweetness of her plan.

On the one hand, it couldn't be more straightforward. On the other, the subtle complexities of it were what truly made it a thing of beauty. So many small pieces working together, everyone guessing at outcomes or making agreements, when in the end, it was all as she'd promised. Just perhaps not quite as some had expected. "You want to know why you have to keep the sheriff alive if you're going to kill him anyway, I assume," she said after a minute or two.

Harm shrugged, either attempting to feign nonchalance or cover his ignorance. Perhaps both.

"I suppose you have earned that right," Anne-Marie said. "You have a rather integral part to play over the next few days. The reason I need you to keep Mr. Rosman alive is quite simple, really. We need him to break away from Travis."

"Ah," Harm said, clearly not seeing the point.

"It's really the oldest trick in the book, sir. Divide and conquer. Right now, we have the whole town against us. My predecessor attempted to peck away at individuals. He wanted to grow his empire one homestead at a time. And, in certain instances, we have known this approach to work. But coming as we are to a field that's been overworked, so to speak, we need a fresh approach. Surely you're familiar with crop rotation."

"I heard of it," Harm said.

"Well, in case you need a refresher, our friends back east are seeing marvelous returns by adding some variety to their farms. A field that is corn one year is beans the next, then corn again the following, and so on and so forth. What they've learned is that fields tire of the same old thing. The soil becomes depleted. A change is needed or the crops become withered, weak. The harvest is smaller. Quite the same idea applies to people.

"One can't simply come in and try the same idea over and over, especially when the field, our town in this instance, is already depleted. The people are tired of being picked at. They don't want to make individual choices. They want unity. Where McFarland attempted to isolate individuals, we are going to give them a choice. They are with the sheriff or they are with the mayor."

"I don't see how going up against two groups is better'n going up against one."

"Ah, Harm," she smiled. "You aren't thinking clearly. We won't be going up against two groups of equal power. We will be up against two groups who are half as strong as they used to be. In fact, if we play our cards correctly, we won't be going up against anyone at all. We let the people make their choices, and then we simply play them against one another."

The man looked down at the toes of his boots, clearly trying to make sense of things. In his mind, he solved problems head-on, no waffling, no clever tricks or swindles. He needed something done, he did it himself. This sounded like putting too much trust in folks who already were on his bad side.

"I see you aren't convinced," Anne-Marie said.

"I just don't see the point," he admitted finally. "All I want is the sheriff. You let me take him out, and that's one less feller you gotta worry about, and I can be on my way."

"Is that what you want though, Harm? Let's say you leave here right now and shoot Chancy Rosman. What then?"

"I ride out, I reckon."

"And to where? Where exactly are you planning to go? Mayor Travis might be a significant nuisance here for us, but he also knows how to be a nuisance elsewhere. Progress is coming, Mr. Swally. Folks don't take lightly to official lawmen being gunned down. A generation ago, perhaps you could've just ridden off to the next town or territory and lived a free life, but those days are behind us. The sooner you come to grips with that, the better off you'll be. What I'm suggesting is we take care of both our problems while keeping our own hands clean."

"You're gonna get Travis to shoot Rosman?"

Anne-Marie laughed. "If only it were that easy. No, I'm afraid Travis, as much as I dislike him, seems to understand the future as well as the rest of us. He could no more murder Rosman than I could. But he can remove him. Shooting a sheriff is one thing, but if you'll recall, shooting another man in self-defense is quite another. Once we get Travis to remove that little star from Rosman's chest, he's just another man. And from what we've both seen, men out here die every day. It's just a part of the life."

Harm finally smiled. "That would make things easier on me. You promise he's mine, though, right?"

"Oh, Harm," she smiled. "The worst thing that could happen is the rift becomes so great that Rosman is forced to take matters into his own hands. From what I've seen that may be a more likely option than I initially expected. But so what if he does? His star is gone. Sure, he can claim to be a bounty hunter again, but no one views those vigilantes as the actual law. Even if by some strange occurrence Travis had the man arrested, what is the worst that could happen? You kill a criminal before he leaves town? Why, Harm, I'd almost say you'd be considered a hero, commended for ridding this place of one more rabble-rouser. You'd be helping clean up the streets."

Harm was positively grinning at the idea. He could really see it. Not only would he get his revenge, but he'd be applauded for it. Maybe he'd even step into the sheriff's place. He laughed at the last thought.

"It's not as far-fetched as you might think," Anne-Marie said, leaning forward across the desk to him. "I've seen it happen, Harm. All we have to do is set the stage and let the men go to it."

"All right," he said after a moment. "Let's say this plan of yours is worth a try. What'm I supposed to be doing to help set the stage?"

"That's the beauty of it." She smiled. "You just keep doing what you're doing. The rest will take its course."

"In a week, huh?"

"Maybe even sooner."

"Well, I gotta say, that sounds almost too good to be true." He hesitated. Things that sounded that way usually were. "But afterward, you're saying I'm in the clear?"

"Harm, if you help me make this happen, you'll be more than in the clear. I don't forget those who step up in a time of need."

"Well," Harm adjusted his hat, feeling comfortably back in the position of power, seeing himself as the one giving aid rather than receiving it. "I reckon I can give ya another week's worth of my time."

"I'd be much obliged, sir," the woman said, smiling over at him.

After Harm had left the office, Anne-Marie's assistant slipped in, sitting in the still-warm seat the man had just vacated. "You're sure about this?"

Anne-Marie grinned. "Now *that* is the truly beautiful part. Whatever happens here next can't help but turn out well for us. If by some odd chance this works the way Mr. Swally is thinking, we've got him in our pocket even deeper. If it doesn't"—she flicked her fingers in the air— "he's one less person to worry about."

Chapter 8
Wainwright's Folly

Harm wasted no time in setting his men after the town with a vengeance. Fires, gunfights, robberies, and hold-ups quickly became the norm, both in and around the town.

Stagecoaches had taken to avoiding the station to the north soon after Swally's men had first been let loose. Now it was almost impossible to convince a driver to take the route.

Word traveled quickly with passers-through and between farmers and their buyers. Just as Elkhorn had quickly gained the reputation as a town on the rise when Frank McFarland had first arrived, the consensus soon became that Elkhorn was a place to be avoided.

Its lawmen were inefficient. Its streets were dangerous. And its mayor was doing nothing about it. At least as far as the regular folks could see.

Travis, once seen as the hope the people needed, a man willing to risk his own neck on the ride to save Teresa, was quickly forgotten and replaced with Travis, the man who had ineffectually tried to rally his own townsfolk against outlaws, the man whose best idea was a signal system that had been ineffectual and dangerous.

Where there had once been a line of folks waiting to share information on the outlaws, there were now citizens grumbling in the restaurants and saloons, becoming more and more certain that the mayor had lost his control. If he'd even had it at all.

Even Chancy had felt the discontent. People with less faith in the sheriff than in themselves had already done more often than not. Shootouts became commonplace as the people grew wary of any outsider, or perhaps became more sensitive to perceived slights.

What they had learned from Frank McFarland, it seemed, was that no one could be trusted, least of all those with power. And the two most powerful men in town had been doing little to nothing to stop the trouble that was slowly taking their quiet town.

And this, Chancy mused, *over the course of three days.*

Amazing how fickle folks could be.

Chancy stood in the main room of the tack shop, smoke and the smell of gunpowder still lingering in the air. A dead man lay at his feet, a pool of blood slowly spreading out from the hole in his chest.

The owner, Mr. Glennings, had his hands on his hips. The revolver he'd so recently used was lying on the counter beside him. Next to him stood a red-faced woman who, though they'd never been introduced, Chancy was certain was the owner's wife.

"Not sure why you bothered to show up now," Glennings said. "Seems to me I did all the work for you. Makes more sense to send the undertaker, get this mess out of the way."

"I gotta file a report," Chancy said, hating to say the words almost as much as he was sure Glennings hated to hear them.

"What is there to report?" the owner asked. "He came in here demanding goods he hadn't paid for. Our exchange became heated, he went for his gun, I shot him. It's clearly self-defense. I have to protect my family, after all."

The woman moved closer as the man put an arm around her shoulders.

"This man threatened your lives?" Chancy said, looking down at the corpse.

"Ask Cheryl if you don't believe me," Mr. Glennings said. "She was here. She saw everything. Isn't that what you need? A witness? Well, here you are. Ask her."

Chancy glanced at the woman, raising his eyebrows.

"It's just like he said," the woman started. "I was afraid for my life. If Charles hadn't had his revolver, why, I shudder to think what could've happened. That could be us lying there now."

The complete lack of emotion in her voice, or at least the presence of only anger, put Chancy on edge. He flipped the dead man's coat open with the toe of his boot. "You said he was going for his gun. I don't see no gun, sir."

Mr. and Mrs. Glennings looked down at the corpse. The man's waistband was clearly exposed, and along with a button from the suspender strap, gun and holster were clearly absent.

"Well, he went for something," Mr. Glennings spat, indignant. "How was I to know what it was? Would you rather I'd waited to see? Perhaps I could've asked him to please tarry a moment until you moseyed by from wherever it is you were?"

"We'd be dead right now!" Mrs. Glennings broke in again. "Lying right there!"

Chancy rubbed a hand over his face. He had spent too many of his hours like this over the last few days. Questionable arguments, drastic outcomes. Folks who seemed to look at him as if he were the problem and not whoever had brought all this trouble to town in the first place.

The worst part was, for every instance like this, even the ones where the motivating factor truly had been self-defense, Chancy spent hours filling out the paperwork, getting the stories written out and filed away.

It's not that he hadn't expected some bureaucracy when he'd taken the job, but the skewed balance wore him down.

Every man had a breaking point, and Chancy was being more and more sure his would come not amid a gunfight but behind a desk with a pencil in his hand.

"Look," Chancy said finally. "Whatever happened, happened. Ain't nothing I can do about it now. You folks claim he pulled a gun. Fine, let's go write it down like we have to. Maybe while we're sitting there, you can settle in and get a good glimpse of why I ain't at your beck and call every second of the day."

The words came out harsher than he'd meant them, and Mrs. Glennings was quick to jump on it.

"Oh, Sheriff, please pardon *us* for expecting *you* to do your *job!* Maybe it would be easier if we just did the paperwork for you as well! Would that be easier?" She huffed, crossing her arms and glaring at him.

Chancy clenched his jaw. He knew folks weren't happy, but he wasn't sure what they expected. He was only one man. Jack had already taken off for the opposite side of town when word had gotten to Chancy about the tack shop.

Clay was at the station and Burl had the day off. Not that it would've made any difference.

Either way, one of them would look into a gunfight up north and one would be stuck here with the Glenningses and their pompousness. "C'mon, folks," he said. "We may as well get this over with."

"And what about this?" Mr. Glennings pointed indignantly at the body. "I suppose you'll just leave that for me to deal with?"

"You happen to be the cause of that," Chancy said through his teeth.

Glennings looked at his wife, an expression of shock on his face that would've been comical in any other setting. "This is what happens when we try to protect ourselves. I'm going straight to the mayor," he said, turning back to Chancy. "This is unacceptable."

"You'll come with me first," Chancy said, turning to the door to keep himself from grabbing the man and dragging him along. "We can even stop by the undertaker's on the way."

Just as the Glenningses protested yet again, a horse galloped up, coming to a dusty halt just outside the tack shop door. Chancy recognized the movements if not the face through the cloud and shadows outside. Jack.

"Chancy!" the deputy threw the door open. "They said you was down here and thank goodness you are. We gotta go. Now."

For a moment, Chancy considered motioning to the body behind him, pointing out that this wasn't the ideal time for a change of schedule. But he also knew if Jack knew where to find him, then the deputy knew why he was there as well.

Whatever was going on, it had to take more precedence than the dead man behind him. And to be honest, Chancy thought, neither the Glenningses nor the body were likely to go anywhere soon.

He turned back to the man and his wife. "You can either stay here or meet me at the station."

"You surely can't be abandoning us with this, this *corpse!*" Mrs. Glennings sputtered out.

"Take it up with your husband," Chancy said. "I'll be back." Then, turning to Jack, he said, "Let's go."

***

When the two men arrived at the scene, a crowd had already gathered. Off to the side, beaten and bloody, a man had been tied to a hitching post, and his hands around the wooden pole were the only thing keeping him from collapsing in a heap.

One of the few men from the patrol both Jack and Chancy had trusted somewhat was currently standing in front of the broken man, a revolver out, though he was careful to keep the barrel pointed to the sky.

Most of the people seemed to have lost interest in both the temporary lawman and the prisoner at his feet. Just on the other side of the street, close to the edge of the wooden sidewalk, a group of mostly women huddled together, murmuring, crying, and cursing. Jack had given Chancy the story on the ride over, or at least the best version available.

The man tied to the hitching post had supposedly been in the saloon across from him, drinking and carousing, typical behavior these days. From what Jack had been told, all had been going along just fine until the fellow ran out of money and wanted to open a tab.

The bartender, one of the few with any sense who Chancy had ever come across had wisely refused and, according to the bartender's tale anyway, told the man he could either go rustle up some cash or hang about and hope for a handout, but he would not get any more drinks until money came across the bar.

No drunk ever likes to hear that, especially not one with a gun on his hip. The bartender told Jack the man had drawn down, but seeing as how he was almost too inebriated to stand, no one had been too concerned. The bartender had hopped the counter, pinned the fellow's arms behind him, and rushed him out of the room, unceremoniously booting him into the street.

"He said he thought maybe that'd been what did it," Jack told Chancy. "Not that he wouldn't serve the guy, but that he booted him out into the road like that."

"Maybe," Chancy said.

"Either way, the bartender said he went back inside. Said he could hear the guy hootin' and hollerin' and carryin' on, but I mean, that ain't nothin' special around here lately. Bartender said he was only worried about keeping an eye on the door to make sure the fella didn't come back in.

"Anyway, the guy's out here raisin' hell for five minutes maybe, threatening to come back with a posse, saying he's gonna bring his boss in, then they hear the shots. Course, everybody hunkers down at that. Don't matter how many gunshots you hear, folks know to get out of the way when the bullets fly. Bartender grabs his gun from in back of the bar, thinking he's really gonna have to run this guy off, so he heads back up front. Before he even gets there, though, he hears the screaming.

"I asked folks who was around, and they said the first couple shots were just up in the air. The thing a guy does when he's making a spectacle of himself, and the way things been, nobody paid it too much mind. Gave him a wide berth.

"Next shot was at the signage up there." Jack gestured toward the wide, thin wooden plank labeling Abe's Saloon. "I could be wrong, but I'm not sure he even hit it. Which is what makes the next part so bad. Susannah Winters's boy comes tearing around out of the alley about then, probably to see what was going on. Apparently, that was the same time this fella decided he was gonna shoot out the front windows of Abe's here. Boy never seen it coming, and if the bullet had gone where it was supposed to, it wouldn't've made any difference.

"Best as I can tell, it caught him just above the ear here." He pointed to the spot on his own head. "I haven't even tried to get too close to that group yet." He gestured to the women. "The saloon emptied like it was God's wrath, though. I got here not long after that, and to tell you the truth, I'm not sure if I wish I was sooner or later in coming."

Chancy looked over at the man tied to the post. The bloodied face was almost unrecognizable as the head swayed back and forth. The man was talking to himself or fighting to stay conscious. Perhaps a little of both.

"What's he have to say?" Chancy asked.

Jack shook his head. "I didn't wait around to find out. It surprised me to see he was even still breathing by the time I got the mob away from him. They'd already had him strung up and I figured that was as good a place as any till I could find you. Plucked Clarkson there off the sidewalk from where he was passing by, stuck a gun in his hand, and made it real clear anybody who got close was getting shot with no repercussions from us."

"You call for the doc?"

Jack gestured with his chin toward a man slogging his way down the street. "Sent a boy after him. Figured no kid needed to be hanging about here, anyway."

Chancy sighed. "You couldn't have at least cut him loose?"

Jack shrugged. "I wasn't really sitting down to map out my options. Tell ya the truth. He looked like he warn't going nowhere, and I didn't wanna waste my time lugging him back to the station before I came to find you. Maybe I shoulda, but I didn't."

The frankness was something Chancy depended on. There was no justification with Jack, no attempts at half-truths or evasive retellings to make himself look better. What happened is what he said, and that was all there was to it.

Chancy aimed his horse toward the doctor and the gunman. The crowd, finally noting his presence, seemed to turn on him immediately. Shouted questions, accusations, and calls for blood all mixed in a harshness of what he had to admit was righteous anger.

He glanced over at Jack, the look being enough to set the man on crowd duty while Chancy made his way to Clarkson's side.

"Preciate ya," Chancy said, dismounting, but keeping the animal between the rowdy townsfolk and their small party.

He pulled a knife from his boot, cutting the rope that secured the man to the post, and glanced between the doctor and Clarkson.

"Doc, why don't you hop a horse and meet us back at the station? I don't think this is gonna be the safest place for you to do your mending." The old man nodded and hurried off down the street.

Chancy looked over at the temporary lawman. "I know you probably wanted to put a bullet in this fella as much as the rest of 'em, and I can't say I blame ya, but thanks for not taking the opportunity."

Clarkson shrugged. "It ain't right."

The sheriff nodded silently, looking around him. How many other folks here would've said that? How many would've believed in it enough to act accordingly? A handful? One? Any?

"Gimme a hand here," Chancy said, and between the two of them, they could boost the weak, barely conscious man up over the saddle.

"Want me to come with you?" Clarkson asked.

Chancy looked over at Jack, who, somehow, seemed to calm the riotous group.

"Might not be a bad idea," the sheriff said. "You were the only one between them and killin' there for a minute. Probably don't wanna try to be too friendly till they cool off."

The man nodded, pointed his revolver back at the sky, and walked on the far side of Chancy as the sheriff led the horse slowly back toward the station in the middle of town.

***

In his office, Chancy, Jack, Clay and Clarkson stood waiting as the doctor finished looking over the patient in a cell down the hall.

"That what you heard?" Chancy looked over to Clarkson.

The man shrugged. "Tell you the truth, I wasn't sure what to think about any of it. Fella was cussin' Abe up one side and down the other, but these days…"

He shrugged again. "Ain't nothing too out of the ordinary. Everybody's kinda coming loose at the seams, ya ask me. I wasn't so much listening to what he was saying as trying to figure out if I should rush him or come after you all. That's when the boy wandered up. After that…" He held his hands out in front of him as if to say, "You know the rest."

"You know that name?" Jack asked.

"Sounds familiar," Chancy said, sitting down on the top of the desk, "but I can't put my finger on why."

Just then, the doctor came up the hall, wiping his hands on a hankie, leaving red smears of blood across the white material.

"Passed out," he said in response to Chancy's raised eyebrows. "I've seen it before, but it never ceases to amaze me. The drunker they are, the more they can take a beating. You get a perfectly healthy fellow. He falls off a horse wrong, breaks his neck, and that's the end. Get him good and liquored up first, and the horse could run a mile with him hanging beneath it, and he'd walk away just fine. I can't say I condone liquor, being a member of the church, but as a medical man, I can't say it has no positive attributes either."

"So he's gonna live then?" Chancy's tone fell somewhere between relieved and disappointed.

"He'll be sore for a few days, that's for certain," the doctor said, "but by the time he's slept off his hangover, much of his other pains will be behind him as well. At least, physically speaking. They said he shot a boy?"

"Not purposefully," Chancy admitted, "though I think you'd be hard-pressed to find anybody who said that makes a lick of difference."

The doctor looked as if he were about to speak and then thought better of it, simply nodding his head and walking to the door. "If you're done with me, I'll be on my way."

"That'll do, I reckon," Chancy said. Then he added, "Hey, you think he's out cold, or can I get him up and talk to him?"

The doctor paused with his hand on the doorknob. "You can try, I suppose. I'm not making any promises, though."

"Thanks, Doc," Chancy said. He looked over at Jack. "C'mon." As the pair made their way back toward the cells, he hollered back to Clay, "Hold down the fort for a minute! But if I was you, I'd lock that door and not let anybody in."

Back in the cell area, a few men dozed. One stared out the barred window. Overnight or weekend stints in the jail had become so commonplace that most looked at it as a kind of vacation from the outside. It was one thing Chancy hadn't expected.

Not all the men were like that, not by a long shot, but the handful he had locked up at the moment seemed to be of a general agreement that time behind bars was going to be the only rest they got for a while.

It was funny Chancy thought. Some folks seemed half-respectable when you got them alone. Other ones weren't so pleased to be taken out of the fun, but a handful of them seemed to treat it like a day off work.

Chancy turned the keys in the heavy door and then looked over at Jack. "You ever get a name?"

"Wainwright. You know him?"

Chancy thought for a minute. "Nah, just another one coming through. Maybe after a bit, we can talk to some of the other fellas in here. This lot ain't been half bad, all things considered."

A moment later, they were standing over the cot where a beaten Wainwright snored away the first few hours of his incarceration. The doctor had done his best to clean up most of the blood.

He'd had to just to get a good look at the man, but the deep gash across the forehead, the broken nose, and the split lip all spoke to a painful recovery waiting just around the bend.

Chancy looked down at the man, wanting to see nothing but a source of information. The rest would take place in court. He had the man locked up, and that was where his say in the matter of the murder ended.

Whether or not he liked it. He kicked at the metal cot with the heel of his boot. "Let's go, Wainwright! Up and at 'em!"

The man's congested snores, due mostly to blood in his sinuses no doubt, changed rhythm briefly, but then resumed their previous steady pace.

"Wainwright!" Chancy kicked at the bed again. "Let's go!"

"Aw, leave him be," a voice called from across the hall. "He ain't going nowhere."

"Can it," Chancy called over his shoulder. "Wainwright! Wake up!" He reached down and shook the man by the shoulders, doing little more than changing the drunk's sleeping position.

The voice from the other cell called out again, laughing this time. "Ya oughtta at least try the right name!"

Chancy looked over at Jack. "Stay here with him."

The sheriff sauntered back out into the main hall, crossing over to where the amused prisoner leaned on the bars, watching the only bit of entertainment that had come his way in seventy-two hours.

"You know him?" Chancy snapped.

"I ain't gonna go that far," the man said, backing up a little and losing his smile. "I seen him around is all."

"Who is he?"

"Look, I didn't mean nothing, hassling you all." The prisoner held his hands up. "But his name ain't Wainwright. It's Blaine," he drew out the pause, "White."

"Blaine White?"

"Easy enough to get confused, I guess," the man said, eyeing Chancy as if to assess any change in the sheriff's demeanor now that he was being cooperative. "Guy can't hardly say it hisself. Always comes out Bwain. Good Lord didn't give him no L's."

"Sounds like you know him pretty well then," Chancy said. "Talk."

"Look…" The man glanced at the other two prisoners, both of whom either were, or were feigning, asleep. "I ain't trying to cause trouble for nobody."

"You already done that," Chancy said. "And I'll tell ya now, the least of your worries is them two fellas and what they may or may not hear. I'm the one with the key to your door."

"Ain't gonna do me no good to get off if all I do is catch a bullet."

"That's what you're worried about? Shoot, that happens all the time here these days. You oughtta know that. You were firing plenty when we come after you. In fact, your buddy Blaine there just put one in a ten-year-old boy not more'n an hour ago."

Chancy watched with more than a little satisfaction as the color drained from the man's face. He took no joy in sharing the news, but the man's reaction belied at least a shred of common decency, which was more than Chancy could say for many of the men who came through.

"You talkin' true?"

"You think I'd make that up? Why you think he's beat half to death? We had to drag him away from a mob. Doc says he don't even know if he's gonna make it."

"He said that?"

"Said he wouldn't make any promises."

The man in the cell paced back and forth for a moment. "Did he mean to? Surely it was an accident."

Chancy shrugged. "Way most folks see it, that don't make no difference. Kid's still dead."

"All right." The man walked up to the bars. "I'm gonna tell you this, but you keep my name out of it. Deal?"

"I don't make many promises either," Chancy said.

The prisoner chewed on the information for a moment, walking back toward the barred window, then up to Chancy again.

"I guess I can't be expectin' you to, neither. So, listen, here's what I can tell ya. Word's been getting around that Elkhorn is up for the takin' now that McFarland's out of the picture. Some people say one group's moving in, some people say another. I even heard rumors about some lady, if you can believe that. All I know for sure is that word's out y'all can't keep up with the trouble, and if a fella's willing to spend a few nights in a cell, there ain't much he can't do 'round here. I don't mean no disrespect, but my experience is that ain't terribly far from the truth.

"Point is, the boss sent out word to round us all up, bring us into town, and cut us loose. I ain't gonna lie. I was onboard with everybody else, but a fella don't go around killing kids or women. Ya gotta have some kind of law."

Chancy glanced at the bars and then withheld comment. He couldn't disagree with the man. It was the way people had been living ever since the push west had begun, and in some ways, it was even slightly more moral. At least the fellow had a code.

"Who's heading this up?" Chancy asked.

"You don't know?"

"I heard some things. I wanna see if what you're telling me adds up."

"If it don't add up, then you better get some new info. Man you're looking for is looking for you too, and he ain't gonna be happy till you've got a bullet in you."

"Him and a lotta others. Who is he?"

"Swally," the prisoner said. "Harm Swally. You oughtta know him. Says you shot his brother."

The tumblers fell into place. It had been years ago, almost two decades. What would bring his past back to him now?

"Look," the prisoner said. "I ain't asking for nothin' special here, just that you don't let on I's the one who told you. I'll take what I deserve from the law, same as everybody oughtta when his turn comes around, but keep me out of the rest of this. It's getting too hot for my blood."

"Yeah," Chancy said, already losing interest in the man. He crossed back over and leaned into the cell where Jack stood over the sleeping Blaine White. "Can you hang around here for a bit? I gotta go see the mayor."

"Course," Jack said. "What about Clarkson? Or this fella, for that matter?"

"Don't worry about him," Chancy said. "Lock the door and he ain't goin' nowhere. Clarkson, well, I guess you two can do what you think is best. I'd keep out of sight for the rest of the day if I were him. He can hang 'round here if he wants to."

Jack nodded.

"Oh," Chancy added. "Keep an eye on this one, too." He hitched a thumb over his shoulder to the new informant.

"He's decided he wants to be helpful."
"You got it, boss."

Chapter 9
Playing Both Sides

"This is absurd, don't you see that?" Mayor Travis looked across the office at Chancy, who simply held his hands out.

"You got a better plan. I'll listen."

"Any plan is better than this." Travis gestured to his desk where Chancy's sheriff star sat gleaming dully in the early evening light.

"This town needs reliability. They need consistency. You're offering them nothing more than what they've expected. I'd had higher hopes for you."

Chancy had been on both sides of negotiations enough times to not bristle at the baiting. He'd let the man say his piece, but that wouldn't change anything. Chancy had decided before he'd walked out of the sheriff's station.

This was more akin to a courtesy call than a request for permission.

"They can think what they want to, far as I'm concerned," he said. "And to be frank with you, the same goes for you. I ain't trying to make any enemies, and you know I respect you and what you're trying to do here. But you out of everybody gotta see I have to do it this way.

"Fella comes into town looking for me, letting all hell break loose just to draw me out… People are dying. I can't just stand around with my hands in my pockets, Travis. A boy got shot today just for walking down the street at the wrong time. I know you got your way of doing things, whether or not you like it. But I can't be hemmed in by your rules anymore."

"I'm not asking you to stand around, Chancy. I'm not asking you to do anything but what you just claimed you want to do!"

"Fine, fine." Chancy pressed at the air in front of him, trying to keep a calm demeanor hoping to settle the mayor a bit as well.

"You aren't asking me to stand around. I misspoke. What you are asking me to do is sit around, filling out forms and running folks in and out of cells like it's a daggone boarding house. That might be what the law requires, and I'd be the first to stick up for the law. Providing somebody else is the one handling that side of things. But this ain't how I operate."

"You never stopped being a bounty hunter, did you?"

"You knew who I was when you asked me to take this job," Chancy said and then grinned. "Which was a temporary position to begin with."

Travis flopped into the large leather chair behind his desk. "You know as well as I do that's never what I wanted."

"A bounty hunter or a temporary sheriff?"

Travis sat quietly for a moment, considering what Chancy had intended as a joke and yet, considering things, seemed to speak more truth than he'd realized.

"I can give you more men," Travis whispered.

"We both know that ain't gonna solve nothing. You already got me and three deputies," Chancy said, sitting down in the chair across from the mayor.

"Men ain't the problem. You seen that when you started your patrols. We got plenty of folks willing to help. Or at least we had."

"We're losing our grip on this place."

"Which is why I'm offering to be the one who lets go entirely. You cut me loose, and I'm just a fella out there on his own again. You know I work best that way anyhow. 'Sides, Jack Wallace ain't going nowhere. We get this all straightened out, and I can either come back or we can just let Jack run the show. He's most likely a better man for this kinda work than I ever was."

"If you come back," Travis said.

It was Chancy's turn to sit quietly. "I suppose that's always something to consider."

Travis reached out and picked up the star, turning it in his fingers.

"I suppose..." He smiled slightly. "We could consider this a temporary leave of absence from your temporary position."

"That'd be one way to look at it, I reckon."

"I'll hold on to this, then." Travis opened a drawer in his desk and stuck the star inside.

"So," he said, looking back up at Chancy. "What do you need?"

The former sheriff grinned. "With all due respect, sir, just for you to stay out of my way."

Travis smiled back. "Like I did with Teresa?"

Chancy stood, extending a hand. "I have a plan."

"Do you?"

"I guess you'll just have to wonder."

The men shook hands.

Just as Chancy reached the door, the mayor called over to him, "Chancy, however you solve this, let's solve it for good this time."

"I'll do my best, sir." Chancy pulled the door closed behind him, already laying out the steps of his plan in his head.

***

Back at the sheriff's station, Clarkson, and Jack Wallace were pacing the office. Clay sat at a chair near the cells. When Chancy walked in, Jack merely raised his eyebrows while Clarkson actually approached the man.

"You got a plan, boss?" Clarkson asked. "I don't mean to be a nuisance, but y'all kinda drug me into this, and I'm not sure I'm in the safest place right now."

"You'll be fine." Chancy brushed past him. "I got a plan for you already. Jack, I got news for you though. Take a seat." Deliberately, Chancy gestured toward the chair behind the desk.

"I was wondering about that," Jack said.

"Figured it out already, huh?"

Jack pointed to Chancy and then to his own chest. "Looks like you're missing a bit of jewelry."

"It was weighing me down," Chancy said, pulling up a chair to the opposite side of the desk he was used to.

"Now look, I got a plan, but I'm gonna need you fellas on my side here. And I mean Jack, Clarkson and Clay. And let Burl know about this when he comes in. Just you four fellas. The mayor's cutting me some slack here, but even he don't know what we're gonna do."

Chancy paused and looked over at Clarkson. "You married?"

"No, sir."

"Got a gal?"

"Well…"

"Good enough, I guess," Chancy said. "I need to know you're not gonna be talking when you shouldn't be. Jack I ain't worried about, on account of his butt's probably gonna be in this chair till everything's said and done. You, though Clarkson, we're gonna have to get real trusting with one another real fast."

"Chancy," Jack broke in. "He was with us."

Chancy raised an eyebrow.

"He didn't linger around much. Might be why you don't remember him. But he rode out with all the rest of us to get Teresa back. He just headed on back when he saw she was safe."

Chancy looked over at Clarkson, who shrugged.

"Figured my part was done, so I headed back," the man said.

"Not much for accolades, huh?"

Clarkson shrugged again. "Just did what needed done."

Chancy smiled. "I think we're gonna be all right then." He turned back so he could look at all three men.

"All right, here's the first thing we gotta do, and listen close cause we ain't gonna be able to just meet up for chats."

***

Back in the cells, the prisoners who were at least awake enough to listen could hear raised voices. What sounded like a chair was tossed against a wall. A scuffle of some sort broke out. A door slammed.

A few minutes later, Jack Wallace appeared at the end of the cell hall, breathing hard, his shirt halfway untucked, his cheeks red. He glanced up and down the cells.

"What?" he yelled, making eye contact with the man who had so recently been feeding them information. "You Barnes?"

"Well, yeah. Yes. Sir," the prisoner said, stepping back from the bars slightly. "Everything all right?"

"Seems like it's your lucky day, then." Jack sauntered down the hall, sorting through the keys on the oversized ring.

"What's going on?" Barnes said, eyeing him suspiciously.

"Apparently, the mayor's feeling real grateful to finally have somebody open his trap." Jack jammed the key in the lock, twisting it to unlock the cell door. "Said to cut you loose."

"No..." Barnes moved farther back in the cell. "That don't seem right."

"You wanna stay?" Jack paused with the door halfway open. "Or you wanna go ask him yourself?"

The man rubbed his palms on his dirty pant legs, unsure how to take this turn of events.

"C'mon," Jack said. "If I was you, I wouldn't be lollygaggin'. You might be safe in this cell for the moment, but once your boots hit the street, I ain't responsible for you no more."

"What's this all about?" Barnes edged closer to the door.

"You need me to draw you a picture?" Jack threw the door open wide and stepped back into the hall.

"Sheriff took what you said to the mayor. Travis said to spring you, since you were trying to be helpful. Sounds to me like he wants a rat, but nobody asked me."

"You may as well put a bullet in me now then," Barnes said. "Swally finds out I talked. He's gonna do it, anyway."

"That's why I'd be tuckin' tail and makin' for the sunset if I was you."

"You can't just send me out there," Barnes said. "You have to protect me."

Jack laughed. "Maybe," he said. "Maybe if I was the one who'd made the deal. But I wasn't. And the man who did just turned in his star."

"You mean..."

"Ol' Chancy didn't much like the plan either, sounds like," Jack said. "Told the mayor the first thing you'd do is run back to Swally and play both sides. Mayor said he trusted you. Why, I don't know. But they had a row. Sheriff came in here and took it out on me. Fact is, if that's the way this place is gonna be, I don't much care one way or the other what you do. I ain't fixing to stick around and find out myself. I've had it. This town's crawlin' with you people, and far as I'm concerned, you can have it."

Barnes looked Jack up and down, still suspicious, but his posture was slightly straighter. His eyes held more confidence. "What about Rosman?" Barnes asked. "What's his plan? He cuttin' out too?"

"Shoot," Jack said. "Who knows with that man? First, he comes in here all hot under the collar because justice ain't bein' served. Next he's tearin' out, hollerin' about takin' Swally out his own self and damn the consequences. Depending on how fast a hand your boss's got, you may've just done him a favor. The lamb's on the hunt for the lion now."

"I heard that sheriff's fast."

"Look…" Jack glanced over his shoulder as if to ensure the other men were still uninvolved. "I don't know how this is all gonna pan out, but the fact is, I may need somebody like you on my side 'fore it's all said and done. All them stories about Chancy, that's all they are. Shoot, McFarland had the drop on him. That woulda been the end of Rosman right there if the mayor and his posse hadn't showed up."

"They can't all be stories," Barnes said.

Jack shrugged. "They may not be. Whether they are or aren't ain't the point, though. The main thing is, Rosman thinks he's that good. But you get him out on his own, he's just another fella with a gun and big ego. If he didn't have half the town on his side, he'da been shot down a hundred times by now."

Barnes rubbed his chin. "That a fact?"

"I been the one working by him all these months. That's the best fact you're gonna get. Now get outta here." Jack gestured with the keys.

Barnes moved a few steps down the hall, glancing back over his shoulder, waiting for the catch. Finally, it came.

"Barnes!" Jack hollered.

The man winced and looked back.

"You remember what I told you?"

"Get him alone, got it."

"Not that part. The bit about me needing a favor down the road. I scratch your back and all."

"You got it." Barnes smiled. "I'll scratch yours."

Jack watched as the man hurried up the hall and through the office where Clarkson and Clay had been instructed to sit quietly and involve themselves as little as possible. Barnes hesitated for a moment at seeing them, then realizing no move was being made to restrain him, he headed straight for the door and out into the night.

Jack walked back up to the office.

"Looks like he bought it," Clarkson said.

"He's a fool if he didn't. I may as well have walked him down to Swally myself."

Clarkson sighed and stood up. "Guess it's my turn to have a go at it." He pulled the brim of his hat down. "Assuming the townsfolk don't find me first."

"They do, you send 'em to me. If ya learned anything just now, it's that, for the time being, you just say what you gotta say and we'll sort it out later."

"You're the boss."

"For now," Jack said.

***

Across town, Barnes settled into a chair in the Shipyard's backroom. Ship himself was out keeping an eye on the clientele and doing his best to prevent another accidental murder while Harm Swally and a pair of his closest associates sat in the back, planning another string of fires for Elkhorn.

"What're you tearing in here like your hair's on fire for, boy?" Swally said.

The low-key demeanor he displayed around the woman had no place outside of her office. In fact, despite what he knew to be otherwise, he liked to tell himself even with Anne-Marie it was just a front, a way of giving the woman the cowering bootlicker she seemed to think she deserved. Out here, he was running the show, and he had no qualms about taking every opportunity to act accordingly.

"I got news, boss," Barnes said, catching his breath. Once he'd been out of sight of the sheriff's station, he ran nearly the full distance to the outskirts, knowing this would be the one reliable place to find his boss or a drink. Luckily for him, he'd found both.

"Take a breath." Swally reached out and poured a shot of whiskey for the newly freed accomplice. "Wasn't a horse to steal between there and here?"

Barnes tossed back the drink and wiped his lips with his sleeve. "Thought about it," he said. "But I didn't wanna risk getting picked up again afore I seen you. Look, things are changing here. And fast."

"How's that?"

Barnes recounted his interaction with Jack Wallace, perhaps embellishing things beyond believability, but at the backroom table, only one thing mattered. Rosman no longer wore the star.

"I'll be damned," Swally said. "Just like she said."

"Who?" Barnes asked.

"An associate," Swally spat. His men knew nothing of who he met with, only that he had connections around the town and some orders came from others. That there was only one other, and that it was a woman no less, was something Swally would take to his grave if he had to.

"So Rosman's a free shot now. What about that other feller? Wallace?"

"He said he's fixin' to cut and run his own self. He's the one told me about McFarland and Rosman and all that."

"And you didn't think that was a little strange?"

Barnes shrugged. "Course I did. I figured he wasn't even gonna let me out of the station. But he kept good on that part. Only thing he asked was that I make sure you knowed it was him who helped me out."

Swally laughed. "That's it? A favor for a favor?"

Barnes eyed the whiskey bottle. "I'm just telling you what he told me. I said I'd do that. Now I done it. And I don't rightly care what you do with it. All I care about right now is cuttin' loose."

He reached out for the whiskey.

Swally plucked the bottle off the table before he could get his hands on it. "Not yet, you ain't. This is the first time you've been pulling your weight around here in a good while, Barnes. I'd hate to kill the streak. Seems to me you're in a unique position."

"How's that?"

"Well, you're in good with the law. Mayhap you could pass along a little information of your own."

"You wanting me to double-cross 'em?"

"I'm just wanting you to keep doin' what you're doin'," Swally said. "You got folks there who listen to what you say. How 'bout you just tell 'em what it is I want 'em to hear?"

Barnes slumped back in his chair. What he'd expected being a night of revelry was twisting into a night of wandering back and forth on the dark streets.

"Now you say Rosman is gunnin' for me, and his buddy Wallace ain't plannin' to stick around. Sounds like the mayor's got his hands more than full just with that mess, let alone what we been planning. Way I see it, a feller like you might let slip just where it is I might be. Rosman comes out looking for me, catches a bullet or three, that only leaves two green deputies, no bounty hunter, and a helpless mayor. We can own this town by the end of the week."

"I reckon that sounds all right to me," Barnes said. "What do you want me to tell 'em?"

"Try this on for size." Swally grabbed a pencil off the table and flipped over a paper that had been sitting there. As the surrounding men leaned in, he sketched out both a map and a plan that he was certain couldn't fail.

Chapter 10
The Leap

Barnes wasn't three sheets to the wind by the time he left the Shipyard, but he had a warm belly full of whiskey and the promise of more after his return.

Things couldn't be simpler. Especially when he happened to almost stumble upon the third man from the sheriff's station. He couldn't recall the fellow's name right away, but it didn't really matter. The man knew who he was, and the man knew Rosman. Those were the only real requirements for a job like this.

Barnes smiled as he righted himself. Maybe he'd gotten a little carried away in his cell before. Swally wasn't so bad, and if folks couldn't keep an eye on their own kids, especially in a town like this, well, it was nobody's fault if something happened. A shame, maybe, but not anyone's fault.

"Barnes, isn't it?" Clarkson asked, helping the man steady himself against the side of a building.

"Didn't catch your name," Barnes said, taking a deep breath and getting his legs under him again. He should've eaten something, he thought. But there was always time for that.

"Clarkson," the man said.

"Clarkson, got it." Barnes tried to remember, as he was sure Swally would want to know.

"Look, Clarkson, I got something I wanna tell ya. I know things ain't workin' out so hot 'tween you all and the mayor and sheriff and the deputies, but I think I can help ya out. You, or at least that other fella, done right by me, and I pay my debts."

"Hey, I didn't have nothing to do with that." Clarkson held up his hands. "That was all the mayor's doing. You wanna pay a debt, you talk to him."

Barnes reached out and grabbed the man's arm as he turned away.

"Look, I ain't askin' for nothing. I'm just gonna tell you the facts. Your pal Wallace said the sheriff's lookin' for Swally, and I know where he's gonna be."

Clarkson felt his heartbeat pick up, but continued the ruse of disinterest.

"That's fine," he said, "but for all I know, Swally sent you here his own self, trying to set something up."

Barnes leaned back. "That's the thanks I get, is it? Swally'd shoot me down right now if he even saw us talking, and he'd worry about whether he should've later on. Fact is whether or not you listen to me ain't my problem. Whether or not you believe me ain't neither, but like I told your friend, he scratched my back, so now I'm scratching y'all's. You don't like it. Well, that's how it goes, I reckon."

"All right," Clarkson sighed. "I s'pose it ain't gonna hurt to hear you out."

"That's more like it." Barnes smiled and put his hand on Clarkson's shoulder. "Now, here's the deal. The reason y'all ain't been able to track down Swally is on accounta he got hisself a place back out past the bluff."

"Faith's Leap?" Clarkson named the cliff in an area to the southeast of town, supposedly named after a woman who'd tested the Lord, or her husband, or simply given up.

"That's the place."

"Get outta here. Ain't nothin' out that way but fields and..." He trailed off.

"And that grove of trees." Barnes smiled. "Best hiding place in the world is the one nobody remembers exists."

"No," Clarkson said. "It ain't big enough. I been out there."

"When?" Barnes laughed again. "I bet not since you's in kid pants. And even if you had been, warn'ta made no difference. Swally just set up camp there within the last twelve-months. But he's smart. He cut from the far side of that grove, built hisself a little cabin in the middle, and left all the rest of them trees up as a screen."

Clarkson had no idea if the man was telling the truth or not. He hadn't been out by Faith's Leap in almost twenty years. Whether any of the rest of the story was true, the one fact he needed was there:

Swally wanted Rosman out at the grove.

"And that's where he's been all this time..." Clarkson seemed to muse, conveniently forgetting to mention that until that very afternoon, until Barnes himself had confirmed it, no one at the station had even the slightest idea who they should've been looking for.

"Clever, ain't it?" Barnes laughed.

"It is," Clarkson said. "But what's in it for you? If I had a boss that clever, I'd think twice about double-crossing him."

"Ahhh." Barnes swatted at the air with his free hand. "That man ain't going nowhere. Clever'll get you some places, but the kind of clever he's got always ends the same way, with a bullet in the back. Not everybody takes to the kind of thinking that man has."

"And you don't neither, huh?"

"Look…" Barnes held his hands out, palm up. "Twenty-four hours ago, you had me in a cell. You know who put me there? Swally. Sure, maybe he didn't lead me in his own self, but he sure enough put me on my way. I ain't gonna sit here and preach at you, and I ain't gonna tell you I'm a righteous man, but I'll tell you this: I'm a man who ain't too keen on sitting in lock-up, and that's what Swally's got waiting for me. Way I figure, you all run him off or lock him up, don't make no difference to me. Long as he ain't at large, things'll be a lot smoother for folks like me."

"Just trying to make your way in the world, huh?"

Barnes's brow darkened. "That's the problem with you lawmen. Never believe a fella when he says he wants to change his ways."

"Can't say as it seems to stick too often, that's all." Clarkson patted the man on his shoulder. "But hopefully you'll prove me wrong. I'll pass your message along."

"And you make sure they know it was me."

Clarkson nodded. "It'll be the first thing I tell 'em, Barnes."

"Well, all right then." The man tipped his hat and wandered back off into the darkness.

***

Chancy sat at the dining room table in the boarding house. Clarkson sat across from him, holding a mug of now-cold coffee, and Teresa, despite his protest, was at his side.

"I have every right to know what you're involved in, seeing as how it has a way of involving me," she'd said.

As much as he hated to admit it, she had a point. Sure, the situation with McFarland was a one-off, but he'd often wondered himself how things might've gone if Teresa had been more prepared for contingencies.

After all, she'd proven herself more than capable of handling everything life had thrown at her so far. And to be honest, he appreciated her being there.

Clarkson sketched out a small map on paper and then made some slight amendments at Teresa's request. She'd taken Betsy out to the Leap off and on over the years and had by far the most recent experience of the place.

"You buy it?" Chancy asked, looking at the woman.

"That he built a cabin there with no one knowing?" Teresa shrugged. "It's possible. Unlikely, I'd say. First off, why would he do that? It's too far away from town to be useful, but it's too close to give him any real safety. The moment anyone saw him hightailing it toward the Leap, he'd only have two options: hide in the grove or take the plunge. Everything else is open fields. I suppose if he built some kind of fort, it could be useful. But again, people know the place. It's not secluded enough to ensure no one would stumble across his hideout."

"So your vote is ambush," Chancy said, "plain and simple."

"If you can think of something else that makes sense, I'd be happy to listen. But if it were me, I'd draw you out into the open like that and then have men positioned all up and down the grove. You won't be able to see them. They'll have the advantage of cover, and they'll see you from a mile away."

Chancy looked over at her and grinned. "You're a bitter woman when you want to be."

"I'm just using my brain." She grinned back. "You should try it sometime."

Chancy laughed. "All right, all right. That's enough out of you. What d'you think, Clarkson? You talked to the man."

The fellow leaned back in his chair. "I'm with the lady," he said. "I don't rightly know if there's a cabin or a house or a darn corral back in that grove, but I know for sure Barnes wasn't gonna be happy till he made it clear that this"—he pointed at the map—"is where you're supposed to go."

Chancy pulled the paper over closer to himself, examining the terrain. "It would be a shame to let him down then, wouldn't it?"

The three sat quietly for a moment, running through possibilities in their minds.

"You know," Teresa said finally, breaking the silence. "There is the possibility that he's simply telling you the truth."

Chancy grinned over at her. "I'll take that into consideration. But just to be on the safe side, let's see what we got for guns."

***

The sun had barely crested the horizon as Chancy, Clarkson, and Jack lay on their stomachs on the far side of the grove. Faith's Leap was off to their left, a fifty-foot sheer drop to a rocky valley.

As Teresa had said, nearly everything else around was empty meadows. The place was sometimes used for pasturing, but also as she'd pointed out, the place was too far from town to be convenient, and too close to be bought up for a ranch.

It was this, rather than the scary story about the cliff, that had truly kept the area as unchanged as it had been over the years.

Between the men and the Leap, a small grove of trees arced across the meadow, making a small southern turn before petering off. It couldn't have been over one hundred feet long from end to end, maybe fifty feet across at its thickest.

Now that Chancy was actually there, the idea of someone building a hideout was not only unlikely, it was laughable.

The trees themselves did not grow thickly. They were a tall, spindly type that reminded Chancy of the aspens he'd seen farther out west.

Combined with the sparseness of the grove itself, the trees were hardly more than a partial wind block, but hardly a screen of visual protection.

Chancy gave his last instructions to the men and sent them off to find secure hiding places, Jack to the right and Clarkson to his left. He was taking a lot of risks with this plan, and were it only him, he might not be so concerned.

But the men had insisted on coming with him, and he'd practically had to convince Teresa to stay at home as well. Thankfully, no mother could argue with keeping Betsy safe, and he'd left Teresa with a promise to return soon. One he hoped to keep even sooner than she expected.

As Jack and Clarkson spread out and dropped from sight, Chancy worked his way closer to the grove itself. The first risk he'd taken had already panned out. He'd been almost sure that Swally and his men wouldn't move immediately.

Odds were they'd wait for Barnes to come back, get the story out of him, gather up whatever posse they wanted, and as seemed to be required for most of the wild guns Chancy had brought down, waste time drinking and gearing up when they could have simply made a move.

Sometimes, he thought, the biggest difference in a fight like this was who had the most patience. Chancy had spent days sitting and waiting for a man to cross his path.

The others didn't seem able to sit still for more than a few hours. It was part of the mindset. The men saw what they wanted, and they took it.

They didn't believe they should have to wait. And it was something that was working to Chancy's advantage yet again.

After he, Teresa, and Clarkson had come up with a plan, they'd sent Teresa out to track down Jack. If anyone had asked, she was on a peace-making mission without Chancy's knowledge.

Once she'd passed on the information to him, she'd returned, and Chancy and Clarkson had slipped out the back door, taking the long way around town to come up on the Leap from the north.

Jack had dipped out of town to the south, working his way over to meet them at the back of the grove an hour before sunup. If nothing else, Chancy was counting on this being to their advantage as well.

True, the sun at their backs would make a perfect silhouette of anyone who stood and become a target, but it would also wreak havoc on the eyes of any man starting into it and trying to take aim.

The only uncertainty was how many men Swally would bring with him. Barnes was a likely candidate, if for no other reason than Swally would want someone around to take out his anger on if Chancy didn't show. But beyond that, he couldn't be sure.

His gut told him the group would be small. A man like Swally wouldn't be confident enough to show up alone, that was certain. But he wouldn't bring so many men that he looked weak either.

Besides, the more guns, the more likely it would be that Swally himself didn't get to put the final bullet in Chancy, and that was something the lawman was sure Swally wanted.

For the time being, though, all he could do was wait. Chancy crept closer to the edge of the grove, slipping between the thin trees and settling himself down behind a small bush, keeping an eye toward where he assumed the men would appear.

***

About an hour later, to Chancy's surprise and relief, the sound of voices and horses could be heard approaching from the northwest. The angle wasn't ideal, but as he crept closer, he couldn't complain about the prompt arrival.

Off to either side, he could detect the faintest rustle in the undergrowth as Clarkson and Jack adjusted their positions to the now visible group. If things went perfectly, they should be able to take the men without a shot.

Of course, when had anything ever gone perfectly?

Chancy counted only six, and from the voices, he already recognized Barnes. That left Swally and four others.

He anticipated little trouble from Barnes, and both Jack and Clarkson knew his focus would be on the leader. Two to one odds with Jack was hardly a fair fight for his opponents, and from what Chancy was learning about Clarkson, the man would have no trouble holding his own either.

The group moved into the grove, slowing only slightly to dismount and lead their horses back away from the edge of the trees. Clearly, they had not even the slightest concern that Chancy could have arrived before them, and even after Swally gave cursory orders to check around, the two men who grudgingly sauntered off couldn't have given less effort to their search.

"Look," Barnes was saying, "we gotta start a fire or something. Make him believe you're really here."

"I am really here," Swally snapped. "You want me to go sit out in the grass and wave to him?"

"I'm just sayin'," Barnes whined. "He thinks you've been holed up here in a cabin. Get some smoke rising. Make him think you're sitting around at breakfast. You gotta be vulnerable."

Chancy smiled to himself. If only they knew how vulnerable they were.

Jack and Clarkson knew to hold back until Chancy made the first move, so he gave the men some time. Even with their lackadaisical attitude, the initial approach would always put men on their guard, at least somewhat.

If he just gave them twenty minutes, enough time to settle in, get their bearings, and more than anything, bolster their confidence that they were the ones in control, the element of surprise would be at its most effective.

Soon enough, acting as if it were his own idea, Swally had Barnes gathering up some sticks and underbrush to start a small campfire. Surprisingly, two of the men actually pulled some breakfast grub out of their saddlebags and hunkered down by the flames.

Swally watched with disgust, but after a few minutes, his stomach got the better of him, and he wandered over to the fire as well, leaving two men to keep an eye on out for an approaching horse.

Chancy shook his head. Amazing.

About ten minutes later, once the food was nearly done, and the lookouts had lost interest in the empty field, Chancy slowly began moving forward.

He still had a small amount of cover as he made his slow approach, listening every few steps for a telltale sign from either Jack or Clarkson. The two men, however, either hadn't moved or were as quiet as a fish in a pond.

Finally, finding a position where two trees grew almost side by side, Chancy stood to his full height and stepped out from cover.

"I hear you're looking for me," he said. "I wasn't expecting breakfast, though."

A tin plate hit the fire, its contents sizzling in the flames, but not before Chancy had both guns drawn.

"I wouldn't," he said, looking from man to man. "Right now, y'all aren't doing nothing terribly wrong. We can head on back to the station and get some things straightened out. Don't need to be any bloodshed."

Swally, as stunned as the rest, was at least quicker to recover.

"What are you doing?" he screamed at his men. "How did you let him sneak up on us? You were supposed to be watching!"

Barnes, as always, was the first to protest, earning him a backhand from his angry boss. Chancy's eyes moved quickly, assessing hands, positions, angles. No one had gone for a gun yet, but that was something he was sure was about to change.

"There's five of you!" Swally yelled. "Shoot him, damn it!"

"Boss, you told us you wanted him," a man on the left of the group said, still holding his plate.

"Take him. There's six of us. He ain't going nowhere."

Swally, red with rage, either at being made the fool or by his own glaring oversight, walked over and knocked the plate from the man's hands. He hesitated just a moment, and Chancy knew this was when something would happen.

"You think that you," Swally said and poked the man in the chest, "can run this gang?" He poked him again, slightly lower.

"I'll show you…" He poked again, this time even lower. "How to run a gang!"

Chancy fired low, hitting the dirt at Swally's feet just as the man made his move, feigning another poke for a quick reach for the outlaw's gun.

"That's not bad," Chancy said. "But you gave it away."

The red in Swally's face edged toward purple.

"Before you get too carried away though, I oughtta tell ya, I ain't the only one out here."

The eyes of the men darted from side to side as first Clarkson and then Jack emerged from their hiding places, guns drawn, and much closer than even Chancy would've guessed.

"Now I'll tell ya again. We can all just head back to the station. Ain't gotta be like this."

It was the last straw for Swally, and Chancy had almost counted on it. He wasn't keen on shooting a man, but he also knew a sick dog needed to be put down. Swally would not let this end peacefully.

In a startlingly quick motion, Swally darted behind the man he'd been poking, shoving him forward with a yell. "Shoot them! There's only three! Shoot them, damn it!"

While ducking for cover, Swally had reached down and drawn his own gun, firing at Clarkson from behind the human shield. The results were instantaneous.

Clarkson went down onto one knee, firing back and dropping the first man as Jack bore down and fired on two others. The movements seemed to slow down as Chancy's mind moved to survival mode.

He saw Jack's shots ring true, blood spurting up from the shoulder of one man, the thigh of the other. Most would've assumed they had missed their mark, but Chancy knew Jack better than that.

They were immobilizing shots, meant to bring the man down but not kill him.

Swally had fallen back, firing wildly as he made for the horses. It was a foolish move in the grove. The underbrush wasn't dense, but it was too thick for a horse and rider to make a quick escape.

Clarkson fired again, spinning the fourth man who'd just now made the choice to go for his gun. It turned out to be a fatal one.

Barnes, the fool, stood directly between Swally and the three lawmen, his hands raised high, screeching something about scratching backs. Chancy squeezed off a shot, just enough to graze the man's arm and get him out of the way.

Barnes hit the dirt, blood running between his fingers as he grasped his arm, howling he'd been shot.

Clarkson darted across Chancy's field of vision, moving in tandem with Jack to close in on the two injured men.

Chancy had just enough time to see Swally pick himself up from the ground, blood darkening the shoulder of his shirt.

Apparently, the shot at Barnes had done more good than Chancy had thought.

The bounty hunter paused momentarily, his mind clicking through options, calculating risks. He looked over at Jack and

Clarkson. The men stood over their captives, Clarkson with his guns still drawn, Jack waving one at Chancy to go, go, go.

He raced forward, leaping over Barnes as the man grasped out at him from supposed agony. "Shut up" Chancy hollered as he ran forward. "You'll live."

Ahead of him, Swally was making a fast getaway. Unfortunately for him, it was in the wrong direction.

Chancy slowed his pace, and followed the man, waiting for Swally to realize his mistake or perhaps, in the sun's glare, race right over the edge of the Leap.

"Swally!" Chancy hollered at the man. "You got nowhere to run!"

Skidding to a halt at the edge of the cliff, it forced the outlaw to realize just that. Slowly, the man turned back to face the bounty hunter, presenting nothing more than a crisp black silhouette against the sky.

"It's funny," Swally said, catching his breath as Chancy slowly closed the distance between them. "I'm no different from you. You killed my brother, Rosman. I came to return the favor. That's justice, isn't it? After all, you're not the sheriff anymore. You're just a man. Just a murderer. No law to protect you anymore."

"I shot your brother, didn't I?" Chancy said, the name finally coming back to him. "It's been driving me crazy trying to think of why Swally sounded so familiar. Well, perhaps I can put your mind at ease then. Your brother, he's the one who was just like you. An outlaw just like you. Tried to kill me, just like you. And spent his last moments staring down the barrel of this very gun. Just like you."

Chancy paused, the sun hurting his eyes, but he needed to keep the man's hands in view. "If you want, though, we can stop this now. Give it up, Swally. You're outta ground."

"So you'd shoot me, would you?" Swally said, now only ten paces from Chancy, and no more than two from the edge of the Leap.

"Take my poor mother's only remaining child? That's cold, Rosman. Even for a heartless bastard like you."

Chancy started to reply when the blurred motion of Swally's hands made the bounty hunter's instincts take over.

The shot rang out clear and crisp across the meadow. Swally stumbled back one step, dropping his gun. A second, clutching at his chest. A third, putting his foot down into empty space. As the woman had predicted, things were over in less than a week.

Epilogue

With the two remaining men behind bars and the help of Barnes leading to the arrest or outright felling of many others from Swally's gang, the head of the snake was, for the time, cut off.

It took some time, but life appeared to be returning to normal, and Elkhorn slowly revived to the quaint, friendly quality it had when Chancy first arrived.

No town in the west was without its ne'er-do-wells, but the number had been drastically reduced. So much so, in fact, Chancy considered leaving the sheriff's star in Travis' desk drawer till the mayor found another man to pin it on.

Old habits die hard, though, and after the days it took getting everything with Swally's gang straightened out, Chancy realized he'd been spending just as much time in the sheriff's station as ever.

He knew Jack didn't need him, but he was thinking he needed the routine, the even pace of a life lived with a purpose beyond chasing outlaws from town to town.

And as was their habit, Chancy brought it up to Teresa one night on the porch outside her boarding house.

"It's a wonderful town," he said. "I'd hate to see something like this happen again."

As she was so adept at doing, Teresa surprised him with her response.

"Again?" she laughed. "Of course it's going to happen again, Chancy. It's the way of the world. There will always be McFarlands to chase down. There will always be men like Swally to take his place. What matters is what you do with that fact."

He sighed. Sometimes—most times—when he wanted her to talk him out of something, she so expertly did just the opposite. "I suppose you're right," he said.

"I'll go see Travis in the morning. See about making things official again." He groaned. "That'll just be more paperwork."

"Oh, Chancy," the woman said, leaning on the arm of her rocking chair to look at him. "That's not what I'm saying at all. Y'know, it amazes me how a man as clever as you can still be so narrow-minded."

"You said it yourself. There's always gonna be another McFarland."

"And there's always going to be another sheriff. Chancy, this is the perfect opportunity. You don't have to be that man anymore. Not only that, you don't have to find someone to take your place. You've got Jack more than prepared to take the star, and Clarkson now has proved himself time and again. With those two in town, backed up by Clay and Burl, I can't imagine anyone foolhardy enough to try to move in. Word spreads in good times and bad after all. Maybe the word was Elkhorn was prime for the picking a few months ago, but I imagine that story is a little different nowadays."

Chancy looked over at her. "You putting me out to pasture?"

Teresa laughed. It was an infectious sound, something that always settled him.

"I'm just saying perhaps it's time you looked at other things."

"I don't know much else besides chasing fellas down."

"Maybe it's time for an old dog to learn some new tricks."

He chuckled. "This old dog doesn't know if he's up to the task."

"Now, that is something I know perfectly well to be untrue. Besides," her voice dropped ever so slightly, just enough to draw his gaze over to her.

"If you're so intent on making something official, I might have an idea."

For the first time he could remember, Chancy was speechless. "You mean…?"

"I could think of worse ideas," she said, looking down at her hands but smiling nonetheless. "On one condition, though."

"What's that?"

"You hang up the guns. I expect a proper husband whom I don't have to worry about getting all shot up every day."

Chancy reached over and took her hand, looking out into the night sky. "You mean to tell me you've been worried all this time?"

She pulled her hand away to swat at his arm, but before she could, he leaned across the small space between them, cupped her chin in his hand, and kissed her in the dark.

The End

Thanks for taking the time to read this story. A positive review on Amazon would be appreciated.

www.ingramcontent.com/pod-product-compliance
Lightning Source LLC
Chambersburg PA
CBHW071749150726
47998CB00005B/1866